Peace Forgotten

ജ

Alethea's Lament
verse 3

Cathryn Leigh

Peace Forgotten

ISBN: 978-1-954413-16-0
First Edition: August 2024

To Tia – If you hadn't passed on your love of reading, I might never have fallen into writing.

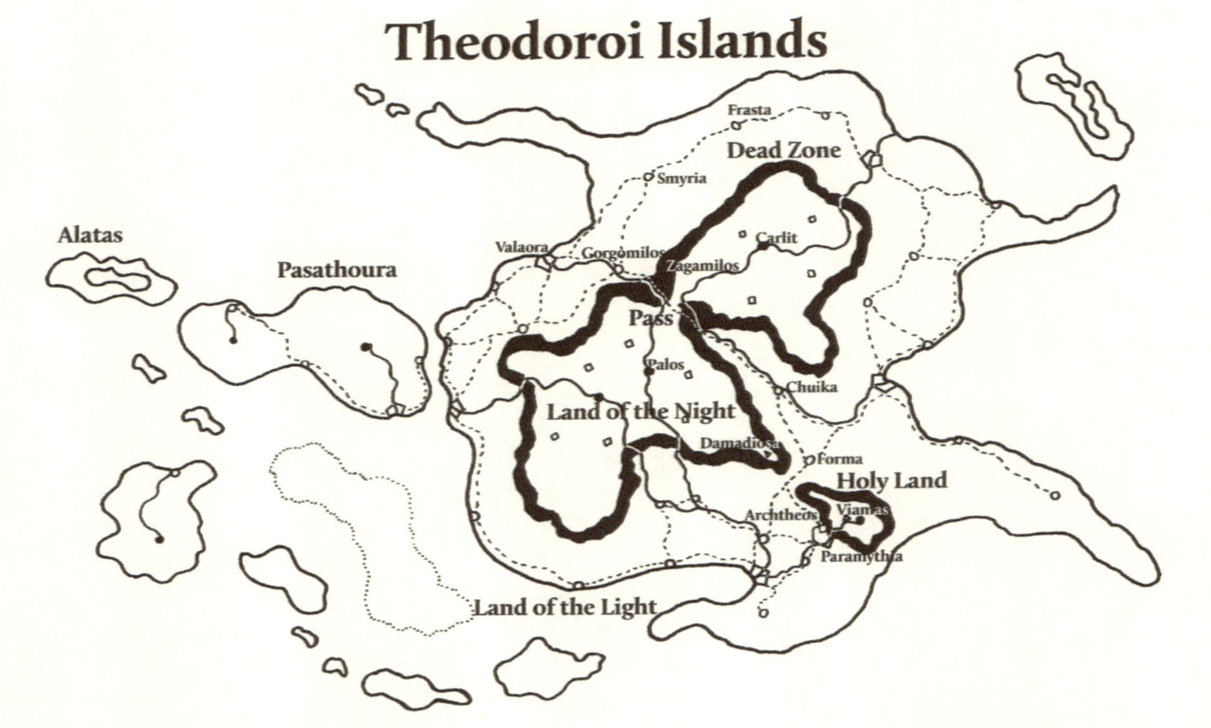

Theodoroi Islands
Alatas
Pasathoura
Frasta
Dead Zone
Smyria
Valaora
Gorgomilos
Carlit
Zagamilos
Pass
Palos
Chuika
Land of the Night
Damadiosa
Forma
Holy Land
Archtheos
Vianas
Land of the Light
Paramythia

Chapter 1

⊰❧⊱

Eramaus sat in near darkness. The torches set in the wall, where no prisoner could reach them, barely lit the hall. Shame, really, that the quake that toppled the Lady's Tower hadn't touched these cells. So there he was, in a dim cell, berating himself for being so dimwitted as to end up there. Then again, how long before he'd have been taken into custody if he'd followed Thea's instructions to protect the Prince?

A voice he'd rather never hear again froze his thoughts.

"Oh, dear," Lowri purred, "what have we down here?"

"Go away," Eramaus heard his cousin, Emelye, respond.

Eramaus shifted his gaze from the cell door to the wall. Of all the people who could have come down to see them it *would* be her. But he barely had the energy to keep the tears back, let alone move. And tears were the last thing he wanted Lowri to see on his face.

"Emelye, Emelye," Lowri chided softly. "Come now, it need not be so bad. Not on you, not on Eramaus, not on any of you." Her voice carried back to other cells.

"How much of it did you orchestrate, Lowri?" Emelye bit

back at her. "I know you've hated Lady Alethea from the day you met her."

"Emelye!" Eramaus was certain Lowri had a hand over her heart as if she'd been stabbed. "How could you accuse me of such things, and in front of others?"

"You've already tried to kill her," Eramaus spoke.

Lowri's plump form, still in the mediki gray of a priestess, gracefully pivoted to face him as Eramaus slowly rose, his anger giving him strength. Once, he had found her irresistible, would have done anything for her. Now she revolted him.

"Twice." He stared into her hazel eyes.

"You too?" Lowri looked at him, hand on her heart, innocent as a hog. "Eramaus, darling," she glided closer, "I think this whole ordeal has addled your brain. Did I not hear you laughing as the Tower fell, crushing the false Lady?"

Eramaus gripped the bars, his face pressing against them. "She was the TRUE Lady of Light!" He squeezed and pulled, as if he could somehow rip the bars apart.

"If she was," Lowri sidled up to him, "then why did the tower collapse upon her? Unless you think there is another way out?"

Eramaus growled, giving his bars a good shake before spinning to face the back wall. He did not want to see Lowri, or speak to Lowri, let alone be close enough for her to touch him.

She emitted a heavy sigh. "I don't think I will understand how such a..."

Her words trailed off and he turned, hoping to see her retreating form. She was still there, her focus shifted to someone in the halls. In the soft silence, Eramaus heard trays being slid into cells. It was close now, but the person delivering them was silent.

A tray slid into the cell caddy corner from him, the one he was certain Emelye was in. His cousin slid it back out.

"You should eat, Emelye, dear."

Emelye snorted. But she didn't slide it out again.

The person pulled a cart into Eramaus's view, carefully avoiding Lowri, who didn't bother to move. The long periwinkle kolobus marked the man as a psara, one of the priests for The Lord of Light. He placed a tray in the cell opposite Eramaus, and, even before Lowri spoke, Eramaus recognized him.

"Tell me, Darian," Lowri purred, "you've confessed to having been led astray. What are your thoughts on whether or not the false Lady could have gotten out of the tower? Do you think your mother knows? She studied under Lady Katica to be the next Lady of Light. But then she had you, didn't she, and you ruined that dream for her."

"My mother wouldn't have told me," Darian spoke softly. "Such things were only for The Lady of Light to know."

Eramaus crossed his arms and glared at Darian. How dare the young man, one Alethea had named as trusted when she became Lady of Light, turn on them.

"Oh, Eramaus." Lowri heaved yet another dramatic sigh as she gazed at him. "Too hot-headed for your own good. Had you stayed with the prince instead of rushing to try and save the shadow fiend—"

"Alethea is not Night!"

"Oh, she is. Lady Katica said so in her journal."

"Beast!" Emelye's bars rattled. "You took it when you were in her tower the day Paladin Ulysses died, didn't you!"

One long stride and Eramaus was at his cell door, grabbing Lowri's chiton, pulling her to him. Darian continued to deliver meals, leaving Lowri struggling against Eramaus's strength as his eyes bored into hers.

"One of these days, Lowri, you will play with a fire you cannot handle." He pulled her into the bars till her eyes begged him to let go. "Beware of what you desire," his voice reverberated in a tone not his own, "lest all your work burn in

Holy Fire."

Shoving her, he let go, his eyes never leaving hers. She stumbled back, breathing hard. Then, with a flip of her braided hair, she snorted and walked out, head high and shoulders back.

Eramaus stepped back till he hit the wall. Slumping, he slid down it to sit on the floor, legs extended.

"Nice try, Lord," Emelye snorted.

A gentle laugh echoed around them as a warm breeze brushed Eramaus's shoulder. *Patience, my children*, it whispered, *your part to play is not yet done.*

Eramaus narrowed his eyes. *He* was very much done with this. Not that *he*'d give a response to The Lord, who never seemed to talk to him when *he* needed it.

He glared as Darian, done delivering meals, passed back though the hall with his cart. The young psara glanced his way, a flush crossing his cheeks. It was hard not to see his finger curled into his pointer where it lay by his right thigh. So, he was still confessing to be a part of the Bleeding Hearts? Liar, if he was, why would he have confessed to having been misled?

Misled indeed. Eramaus pulled his tray of food toward him and began to eat.

"I wouldn't eat it," Emelye stated. "She probably poisoned it."

Eramaus stopped, hand halfway to his mouth, staring at the food. Shrugging, he finished the motion, stuffing it in his mouth. "I'll die this way or die by public execution, what's the difference?"

Emelye sighed and he heard her tray move. "Public execution? That *would* get her off."

❧

Eramaus's bet was on public execution, but Agamedes and a psara he recognized from the midnight Bleeding Hearts meeting thought it would be hard labor. Frankly, Eramaus would prefer to be executed and have it over with. That would certainly suit his inability to do what was asked without destroying something.

Like the way he'd destroyed his relationship with Thea, twice now. Once when he nearly drowned her and once when he'd refused to see that she really had been called upon by The Lord.

He picked at what he figured was breakfast. They were all silent that morning, which was fine with him. He didn't need anyone trying to tell him Alethea was alive, when he'd seen a whole tower fall on her.

But his solitude was interrupted by the footsteps of guards. Well at least it wasn't Lowri come again to torture him with her words. He should have killed her when he had the chance.

"Come on, plenty of work for you," the burly man at his bars stated.

Eramaus grunted and stuffed what was left of breakfast into his face. Two men came into his cell and Eramaus entertained the idea of trying to break free and running. But he caught Emelye's eyes as they took her out. What would he do when he got out anyway? Not like he had anywhere to go. Joining to become a Squire meant you gave up all rank to serve The Lord and Emperor. Not like his father would want him back. Maybe he *should* go to the Land of the Night. They'd kill him or enslave him. Maybe he'd learn how to follow orders better that way.

Still, the moment they ascended to street level the urge to flee rose once more. But where *would* he go? If only Thea had agreed, before they'd arrived in Archtheos, to run away with him. If only he'd stayed with the Prince instead of running into a battle he couldn't win. If only, if only…

He squinted as they turned from the shade of the palace walls to walk along the walls of Archtheos. Their path made Eramaus realize how strategically placed the prison was between the Palace and Archtheos. Maybe he should run, so they could shoot him in the back and end his misery. Glancing back at him, Emelye stumbled, as if sensing his morose thoughts. Fine, he'd live, for now.

Now that they were on the proper road to Archtheos, people passed them going both ways, barely noticing them. Was it not yesterday that the ground had shook and the tower fallen? Was it not odd to see men in the kolobus of a squire in chains? Looking up, he could see the Basilica Spire. Intact. His gaze went back to the unfettered people. No concern. He didn't expect an uproar, but for The Lord's sake, they'd lost their Lady of Light, and her tower. The Tower that had stood for over five hundred years, gone. How did that not cause a stir?

They did know, right? How could they not know? Surely, they had felt the ground shake. Surely, they could see, just as plain as he could, the empty spot where the tower should be.

THEA, his heart sobbed.

He was so stupid. Why had he not listened? He could have been keeping Prince Lyrcus safe. Why did he not listen?

Your heart is strong. The wind ruffled his hair. *Fear not, there is redemption for you.*

"Redemption my left buttocks," Eramaus muttered, causing a whip to crack in his direction. He glared at the ground.

When his eyes flicked up to the Basilica, Darian caught his gaze. The young psara waited for a man to finish drinking from a jug. He snarled at the boy. *TRAITOR,* he thought as loudly as he could at him. Darian either ignored it or wasn't aware, because he still made the Bleeding Hearts gesture by his thigh as his foot etched the dirt.

Wait.

Wait for what? Execution? Interrogation? It better not be wait to confess how Eramaus had been led astray. If anything, *he* was the one who'd kept trying to lead Alethea astray. And here he was, paying for it. That much he was sure of.

But by the time Eramaus thought to look back to Darian, the young man was taking his jug to the next worker. Whatever Eramaus needed to wait for, he hoped it would be soon.

The rope jerked Eramaus forward again, and he noticed that Emelye was being led off in a different direction. Why couldn't he just die and be done with it? *Why am I still alive? Thea is dead!*

But there was no answer. Stupid God only answering what He felt like answering.

Well, Lord of Light, you better have taken Thea into your care and Illumine her, because out of everyone, she deserves it the most.

His eyes sought the Holy Land where it lay hidden above the black rocks of the Dead Zone that separated the People of the Light from the People of the Night.

"Ah, good." Paladin Poulos's voice brought Eramaus's eyes to the rubble before him. "I see our false Lady's champion has been brought to work."

Eramaus growled at the man, knowing he shouldn't.

Poulos laughed as he leaned in. "I hope you find your false Lady's body." His quiet words were vicious. "That is an expression I *will* relish."

Poulos straightened and walked away, leaving Eramaus staring at the mess that had been a tower. A few others, prisoners like him, were already clearing the rubble. It was a haphazard pile, but there were groans and calls for help from it. Eramaus grimaced. Rescue those who tried to take Thea from him, from everyone? The very idea rankled his soul.

"Did you not hear the Paladin?" A guard shoved Eramaus toward the other prisoners. "Get to work and help get those survivors out of there!"

If it wasn't for the directed command, Eramaus would have started clearing rubble the furthest from the pleas for help. Instead, he navigated around the tower to the others, constantly aware of his watcher. The rope connecting his four limbs limited his movement, and more than once he stumbled and nearly face planted.

They'd found a hand, and, grumbling, Eramaus helped shift the rocks away. He didn't want to. Everyone in the tower should die. They had all attacked Alethea. But, his eyes glanced to the Holy Land, to the back rocks that the tower had been built against. Thea would have told him that it was not for him to decide their fate.

He looked down at the arm he had exposed. "This is not for you," he muttered, "not because anyone is making me," he hefted another rock off the pile, "but because it is the *right* thing to do in memory of Thea Lady."

Eramaus snorted at the irony of how his might was making things right. He plugged away, the others quickening the snail's pace he wanted to work at. Not that their pace was satisfactory to the guards either. More than once, the whip lashed out with the call to work faster. Most often, it was aimed at Eramaus. Conversation between the prisoners was restrained, except when needed to coordinate removal of debris.

Glimpsing Darian, still unfettered, annoyed Eramaus. But his stomach rumbled for the food he'd delivered. Not that Eramaus and the others were allowed to eat and drink until the first man was free.

Emelye, still fettered, followed another mediki to the rescued man. Eramaus swore Emelye's mediki supervisor was a Bleeding Heart. The two of them eased the man's pain before four psaras came to take him on a blanket sling to the infirmary.

The guards herded Eramaus and the others back to work the moment they had finished eating. Until the guards came to tie them all back together at dusk, he'd wondered if they'd be at it all night. Pausing by the infirmary, the guards roped Emelye back in with a second mediki.

Back in the cell block, they ate under the watchful eye of Paladin Poulos. The man strode the corridor, stopping at each cell. "I can tell by your eyes," he spoke as he faced Eramaus, "that you have yet to find the body I am looking for."

"What's the point in finding a body, if you already know she's dead," Eramaus spat at him.

"No matter, you *will* be back at it in the morning. A small penance for your traitorous actions."

෨෬

Pain greeted Alethea as consciousness tried to return. Moving only intensified the feeling. It shot from her legs through her back. Her head throbbed, eliciting a groan. Her parched lips were barely able to part as she whispered, "Why, Lord? Why?"

But The Lord of Light was silent. Memories of how she got there rushed in with agonizing details. Alethea gulped. They'd attacked her outright. The people she was supposed to be helping, healing, had attacked her. A hot tear ran down her cheek and she closed her eyes. Why should she live? All those who cared for her likely thought her dead.

Her thoughts flew to Eramaus. Was he alive? Did The Lord still protect him as He promised?

But then again, what good was her promise to be The Lady of Light, The Lord's Bride, when the People of the Light had

9

rejected her.

Death would be kind.

Voices drifted to Alethea and she blinked open her eyes. Figures crossed the Holy Land. People of the Night. One looked at where the waterfall had been, the other scolded, hitting him on the shoulder. Looking away he rubbed the spot. When his eyes found her, he shouted and ran forward. The other caught up and passed him.

Alethea studied the woman's face. Her lips pursed as her brow furrowed. Alethea wanted to beg for death, but the only words of their language she knew were the ones she was taught. The ones she used to request the Light be able to come to the Holy Land.

"~I am The Lady of Light,~" she croaked.

The woman placed a finger to her lips and barked at the man, no boy, who came up. Alethea vaguely remembered him. He knelt beside her, eyes wide. He looked to the warrior woman and spoke. Alethea could hear the concern in his voice. The woman argued with him. At first he talked back, all the while gently touching Alethea's body, quickly removing his hand when she winced. At last, he sat back, looking to the woman. Alethea couldn't move her head to see the warrior, but she heard the stern command in her voice.

The boy sighed and stood. "~Lady of ~ something ~Enlighten-us,~" he grumbled, earning another hit to the shoulder. Rubbing his shoulder, he frowned, and took off across the Holy Land.

The woman stepped into Alethea's field of vision, crouching before her. She caught Alethea's eyes in her stern gaze. "Remain where you are and cause no harm. I will return."

The rehearsed words, spoken in Light, stung. How was Alethea to go anywhere when pain clouded all things? Her legs were stuck, any movement of them shot pain into her skull, which threatened to explode. She wasn't even sure she could

move her arm. It lay stretched out, pleading to the statue of
The Lord.

The woman sighed, muttering something in the language
of the Night as she moved away.

Alethea hoped the boy had been sent to fetch their Gran
Mamara. The elderly woman would be a friendly face, and one
who spoke Light.

Something shifted as the out of sight woman of Night
grunted. A rock flew past Alethea's field of vision. Muttering
in Night, between the grunts, the woman continued to shift
rocks. As the pile grew bigger before Alethea, the pressure on
her legs lessened. The release replaced the dull pain with an
agonizing one. Her legs were broken. She had no doubt. And,
Alethea remembered, there was an arrow in one.

Please Lord, take away this pain, she begged silently. *Please?*

Her plea was partially heard, for she vacillated between
darkness and light. In the darkness, there was peace. In the
light, pain. Yet she was vaguely aware that more Night had
shown up. They called to each other as rocks were moved.
Their words were garbled and odd, yet there was a comforting
familiarity to them.

Alethea faded back into darkness until a sharp pain shot
up her leg through her back, splitting her head.

She screamed.

Hands gently stroked her hair with soft whispered words
of comfort. Alethea blinked, seeing the face of the boy from
before. The name came to her. Toli. He'd mended her before.
The day she'd been stabbed, here in the Holy Land. *Why Lord?*
her heart cried, but the wind barely stirred about her.

A male voice near her feet spoke in a commanding tone.
Toli nodded and reached for a canteen. It was oddly embel-
lished. Toli adjusted Alethea so that she was more seated. The
thought that it might be poisoned crossed her mind as he
placed the canteen to her lips, but what would they gain by it,

other than possible war?

She snorted at that thought. The Light tried to kill her, why would they care if she went back to the Night? They thought she was one of them anyway.

"Drink," the familiar voice of the Gran Mamara spoke as she crouched next to Alethea. "It will ease your pain."

Alethea drank, nearly spitting out the first sip.

The Gran Mamara chuckled quietly. "Yes, it does not taste well. Take small sips."

Alethea did as she was told. The Gran Mamara stood, her voice going from soothing to commanding. She demanded answers to her questions, hushing others when Toli's voice began to speak. There was another voice Alethea thought she'd heard before. Other voices chimed in, starting an argument among them.

"~Celenci!~"

The Gran Mamara's single word quieted them all. She crouched down, looking at Alethea's tear-streaked face. She nodded to the man at Alethea's feet, and he yanked her leg bones. She screamed again with the pain, nearly falling back into unconsciousness. Toli once more offered her the canteen. She drank deeply from it, hoping it might offer her oblivion.

Placing a gentle hand on her forehead, the Gran Mamara spoke. "You are very injured. It will take weeks to walk again and months to fully heal. You may stay here, and we can send a message,"

"No," Alethea cut her off. "No," she spoke more softly, trying desperately not to sob. "They do not want me." A sob broke through. "They would kill me."

"~Sill Er?~" The young woman whose voice she recognized stepped forward.

The indignation on her face reminded Alethea of Eramaus. And the Gran Mamara spoke in Night to the others, setting off a round of hushed whispers. Someone asked a question that made the Gran Mamara laugh sadly as she answered in the negative. Indignation spread to more faces.

"Lady Alethea," the Gran Mamara addressed her again. "The earth shaking has come from your Lord of Light, has it not?"

Alethea blinked. Pain still laced her thoughts, though the drink had banished it to a steady throb. She took a deep breath and let it out.

"Yes. They," she paused, "they have not chosen, wisely."

"They chose you to be their Lady, did they not?"

Alethea's throat tried to close around the words. "Lady Katica," she swallowed, "and The Lord chose me. The others," she gulped, "they do not like me. Nor," a sob escaped her throat, "do they want me."

"And what of the one whose quick thinking saved you?"

Alethea closed her eyes, tears trickling down her cheeks. "I don't know. Eramaus was outside when the tower fell. But," another sob escaped, "they probably killed him for supporting me, trying to defend me."

Alethea felt a touch on her head. Her eyes opened to see the Gran Mamara stroking her hair as she spoke once more to the group. She was surrounded by the warriors, but unlike her vision dream, they did not point their spears at her. Sobs welled in her chest. They hurt, but the Gran Mamara's kind voice was like Lady Katica's, like the voice of the mother she lost when she was five. Trying to be The Lady of Light isolated Alethea, despite Emelye's and Darien's, and even Eramaus's, attempts to be there for her. Yet here, with these strangers of the Night, she felt connected.

All Love, the wind whispered, caressing her with its warmth. The voice was both male and female, kind and hard.

Alethea tried to pull herself together as the Gran Mamara stood. Toli gave her more drink and something to eat. Alethea's consciousness began to softly fade as they placed her on a woven mat suspended between two poles. The man who had been at her legs switched with Toli and four women picked up the poles to carry her.

They sang a song that woke odd memories in Alethea, but consciousness slipped away before she could grasp them.

Chapter 2

⚜

Bit by bit, Eramaus and the other prisoners cleared away the rubble. At least three of them had been trying to stop the attack on the tower. He didn't know them. They hadn't been there when he'd been initiated into the order of Bleeding Hearts. Not that it mattered. Thea was gone, so what good was a society meant to protect her supposed to do. Their purpose was gone. His purpose was gone. Yet there he was, moving rocks from the pile that was once a tower, to a pile that, who knew what was going on with it. He just knew other men sorted through it and carted it away.

Despite trying his best not to care, Eramaus kept track of the days. They had found three men alive in the first four days. On day five of this toil, they found their first dead man. It had taken three of them to lift the stone that had crushed his chest. He'd died one arm across his face, head turned to the side, sword arm pinned above his head.

"I hope you suffered," Eramaus muttered as they carried the body to the waiting stretcher.

Emelye wretched at the sight and he felt a tinge of sorrow

for his cousin. She was not meant to be a healer, though, as far as he knew, that was all mediki did. He knew she wasn't aiming to become a wife to a Knight or High Psara. She didn't like men that way.

Eramaus heaved another stone, nearly toppling with the effort. He noticed the others had also started to wane. The bread and gruel they were fed certainly wasn't enough to keep them in shape. Maybe this was how he would die. Worked to death. Rumor was the palace was built on the bones of prisoners like him.

Had the tower been built the same way? If so, Alethea should never have been The Lady of Light. And if she'd never been The Lady...

"UUHh," Eramaus grunted , throwing a rock on the pile, just missing the guard.

How much longer did Darian expect him to wait. And what was he waiting for? A miracle that would right all wrongs? He snorted. Probably for his interrogation followed by a public execution.

But as much as he wanted to lay down and call it quits, his body wouldn't. He found some delusion in thinking that by escaping he could make them pay. His mind raced with options, from a fight in the jail cell to just running while outside. But he was always bound, the ropes barely giving him freedom to move around the rocks. Getting a knife from a guard would mean a fight. And a fight meant blood, and blood was how they tracked a dying animal.

Even if *he* got free, he couldn't leave Emelye. She was the closest person to Thea he had. And where would they go? Above the Dead Zone? Oh, Emelye'd probably love their women warriors, probably become one. But what was he going to do? Overthrow whoever was in charge to make *them* attack the Light?

Eramaus hefted another rock, slumping. He carried it over

to the pile, barely missing his feet as he dropped it. No, none of that was an option. Thea would be disappointed he'd turned to violence.

He hung his head, plodding back, ignoring the whip crack in his ear. No, he had to wait. He squatted to pick up the next boulder.

Lord, he thought, *What in the Ocean am I waiting for?*

Patience, a soft breeze whispered in his ear. *Patience.*

Eramaus lifted another boulder, screaming out his frustration.

❧❧

The next night, rain pounded the street above and Eramaus sighed as sleep evaded him. He'd heard the Paladin discussing how the Pilgrim's Path had been blocked by tumbling rocks and a steaming fissure. Served them right to have their access to the Holy Land cut off. Why was everyone saying it was the 'false Lady's' fault? Not like Alethea would have prayed for it. The Lord was capable of doing it on his own. After all, hadn't Thea told him The Lord had warned her that He would show His displeasure when Poulos was anointed paladin. And why were they looking for a way into the Holy Land? Did they think she'd survived?

A sob threatened to wrench itself from his chest. But there was no way he was going to let it out. Not when the guards and other prisoners could hear him. Just one day at a time. He had to take one day at a time. If only he could shut his brain off. But that was nigh impossible. Around and around it went, from dreams of Thea being alive only to be killed by the Night, to visions of her mutilated body beneath the stones. The worst was the nightmare of finding her alive only to watch Poulos have her drawn and quartered.

He bolted awake at that one, a scream dying on his lips.

A tray slid into his cell, and he looked up to see Darian at the door. The young man regarded him with concern, but quickly turned from his scowl. Eramaus was not about to trust that man with his troubles.

When they broke for lunch that afternoon, Emelye managed to sit next to Eramaus. She passed him something with the food.

"That's not food," he hissed at her, looking at the stem and tiny leaves.

"No," Emelye whispered back, "it is herbs for your health and strength."

"How'd you get them?" Eramaus narrowed his eyes.

"Darian."

"That traitor—"

His words stopped as Emelye laid a hand on his, holding his fist closed around the herbs he wanted to toss. "I know you don't know him like I do, but trust me, he's still on our side. He told me they've called in the High Psaras. Hopefully Perroa can knock some sense into the group."

"Isn't *he* in Lady Katica's book as a Bleeding Heart?" Eramaus raised his eyebrows. "I'm surprised Poulos hasn't brought everyone from Lady Katica's book in."

"Eramaus, eat, and take those herbs." Emelye glared at him. "Your life isn't over."

Eramaus glared back. He should have asked if Prince Lyrcus was in danger. If his life wasn't going to be over, maybe he should figure out how to protect the Prince. Not that his older, half-brother, Prince Sarpedon, would let Eramaus near the boy.

Pouring out his frustration heaving rocks, Eramaus was thankful he found no one.

Chapter 3

ഇ)യ

Alethea faded in and out of consciousness. She was on some sort of bed, a woven matt, but it was not on the floor. A light blanket enveloped her, like a babe in swaddling. Waking brought pounding in her head, and a moan, or sob, to her lips. Sobbing hurt. But the sound would bring Toli to her bedside and he would speak something. It sounded so familiar, ending with enlighten-us, the way a Light prayer ended with Illumine-us. He would help her eat and drink that bitter beverage and she would sink back into unconsciousness.

Sometimes she would be awake without really being awake, barely noticing, and yet seeing all the details of the place she was in. A window high above her bed gave enough light to see the woven roof above her. There were others in there, all of them tended by men. Only Toli came to her bedside. Odd that for the Night it was the men who healed, like mediki, and the women who fought, like squires. But thinking of mediki and squires made the tears flow and her heart ache.

She sobbed, turning to where Toli came from, welcoming

the relief his drink and food gave her.

"Need rest," he spoke in heavily accented and broken Light. "Body must mend. In few days, we check, see how you mend."

Or had he spoken in Night? The thought ran through her mind as she passed into darkness.

A voice sang in the darkness, the face an indistinct blob in her memory. A woman, a mother, her voice stopped, a male voice tried to pick up the tune, stumbling over the words. The woman's laugh was soothing, the man's jovial. Her voice sang again, until the darkness enveloped Alethea in a blanket of love.

All Love, whispered about her, a duet of voices. *Parent and child, lovers together, friends forever, family found, all Love.*

Friends? Lovers? Parents she'd never know? The anguish in her chest ached greater than the pain in her legs. She wanted to cut her heart out, to not let anyone else into it. It was painful, she'd be better without it. But without it there would be loneliness. She remembered loneliness and the deep sadness and numbness that came with it. It had been brightened with Eramaus and their childhood adventures. Brightened by the blossoming of friendship with Emelye. And even when Eramaus and she had broken apart over her promise to The Lord, she knew he would always be there.

And where is he, Lord? her heart cried out. *Where are they? Those who thought me worthy? Have they been punished by those who hunted me?*

Hush child, a powerful feminine voice responded, *you are among my people now. They are your people too.*

And, The Lord's voice joined The Lady's in unison, *your work will help them understand they are our people.*

A sudden chill brought Alethea to with a jolt. Her blanket had been removed, leaving her exposed to the air, though she was oddly wrapped. A man methodically unwrapped her legs from their bandages while Toli stood nervously at her head. He looked toward someone in the door.

Turning her head, Alethea saw Juana, the girl who had introduced herself the first time Alethea had taken the Lady's Path to the Holy Land.

The Lady's Path.

Her breath caught.

Toli asked a question, the man at her legs replied in the negative. The words were almost intelligible. Alethea tried to focus on what the man was doing. Tried to use that as a distraction from the horrible memories that crashed into her mind. The man bent her leg, rotating it, making her wince. She winced again as he did the same to her other one. He nodded with a look of satisfaction, and, giving an order to Toli, he walked away. The boy went to the end of the bed and began immobilizing her upper and lower leg separately.

When he was done, Toli held his hands above her legs. "Lady of Night," but his next words she couldn't catch, then "Ah-lee-tia's legs,"—at least she thought it was legs—then there was something else and finally, "Enlighten-us."

Enlighten-us.

It was clearly the end of a prayer, but there was no warmth or tingling that came with it. She took the drink he offered, nodding though she only understood the words rest and soon.

📍

Alethea found herself more awake than she had been, and wishing she wasn't. Thoughts whirled around her mind. She didn't even understand why she was so hated. If Lady Katica had not pronounced her as The Lord's Bride, things could have been different. Maybe they would have just let her be an ugly mediki. Too thin and looking too much like the Night to be worth anyone's time.

The Gran Mamara never came inside, though Alethea sometimes heard her voice. In fact, the only women inside were injured. More often, she would hear Juana speaking to Toli. Once she saw them in the doorway, but as soon as Alethea tried to catch Juana's eyes she walked away.

They are your people too, the voice from her dream echoed in her head.

Her people.

Born of the Night, blessed by the Light. That phrase too would never leave her. A line in a prophecy, a line spoken to her when she wondered who she was.

Had her mother taken on a Night lover? No wonder Alethea's father hated her. She couldn't be his, not if she was half Night. Unless *he* had taken a Night lover. But then why would her mother have loved her so much if she wasn't hers.

Alethea shook the thoughts from her head. Maybe she wasn't born from either of them. What had Lady Katica said? 'I doubt that child made it home.' Had the mother she'd known stolen her from her true parents? Alethea could have had a different life. But then she would never have met Eramaus and Emelye and Darian. A sob shook Alethea's body.

She tried to keep it in. She was the only one in here who sobbed, or cried out. These women of the Night, even when injured, were strong. They didn't wake up sobbing. She hadn't even heard any of the injured men carry on as she wanted to. But she couldn't stop it. Her life was upside down and inside out. If only she'd taken Eramaus's offer to go north, to hide, and just live like normal people.

But then, then Daphne would be Lady of Light and Lowri would be the Empress. That wouldn't have mattered would it? There would still be peace.

But her gut said no.

Alethea sat up. She needed to see the sunrise. Needed to know the world hadn't gone up in smoke and flames. Otherwise, what was her purpose here? Why should she survive when she ought to be dead? How do you bring two people together, when one of them wanted to kill you? And why, if Eramaus *couldn't* be her reward, should she even try?

Love, the wind whispered its voice masculine and feminine at the same time.

Yeah, well, it would be nice to feel loved, again, Alethea snapped as she used her hands to bring her legs over the edge of her odd bed, one at a time. Grabbing hold of a cross pole in the wall, she pulled herself up. Little by little she rose. She brought her other hand to the wall as her legs felt the need to buckle.

CRACK!

The pole she held onto broke, and she tumbled to the floor with a cry. People in beds rustled as they sat up, their heads turning toward Alethea. Her face flushed and she desperately tried to get herself back onto the bed.

"TOLI!" The giant young woman on the bed next to her yelled.

Alethea caught the words *butt* and *walk* in the next sentence she spoke. The woman then swung herself out of the bed. Her chest was wrapped in a bloody bandage. She grinned at Alethea as she helped her back onto her bed.

"Coleta," she smiled, offering a hand to Alethea like Juana had.

Alethea took it. "A, Alethea."

The woman squeezed her hand with a shake before letting go and moving back to her bed. She winked and said something that Alethea caught most of.

"Don't tell (something) or (something) stay longer."

Toli appeared not a moment after Coleta had settled herself. He studied the big girl with a frown. She just grinned and winked. He sighed and gave her a half-hearted admonishment that echoed what she'd just told Alethea. He then turned his attention to the broken wall.

Heat rushed to her cheeks and Alethea hung her head. "Sorry," she muttered.

"Coleta's done (worse?)." Toli looked to her. "I (can, will?) fix."

Alethea blinked at her understanding. As if she'd somehow remembered while she was sleeping. But why would she have known Night. Lady Katica had barely taught her anything.

"Stay in bed," Toli's voice broke her thoughts. "I get crutches."

The words felt broken, like Alethea was missing pieces of the puzzle. She'd heard 'stay in bed' often enough. The women in particular liked to get up before they were declared healed enough to leave. Coleta being a good case. She wondered what had happened to bring the woman into this place to begin with.

Alethea blinked as she finally thought to put the details she'd observed together. The hut was six-sided with poles the size of her wrist at each corner. They arched up, weaving a star at the top before arching back down to the other side. Two doors stood opposite each other, with beds evenly dotted about the structure. Windows started at about shoulder height to just above head height, and they had odd overhangs, propped up on the outside.

Toli came back, with what Alethea presumed were crutches. Juana followed him, stopping at the door. Toli helped Alethea settle the crutches under her arms. They gave her stability so she needn't put much weight on either feet.

She was probably well enough now to call upon The Lord to heal herself, but, she glanced around, even in the infirmaries of the Light, mediki didn't do that. Not the way she did. It was just one more thing that set her apart. She would suffer with her broken legs, a penance for failing to keep the Light from poor choices. Choices she should have been able to influence as Lady Katica had. Choices that played into ambition, not into the wellness of the people.

Alethea winced as she bumped into the last bed before the door. Juana stepped aside, letting Alethea swing out of the walls that had surrounded her for who knew how long, and into the dawn of a new day. She stopped to look toward the lightening sky in the east.

Lord of Light, she thought, not wanting to utter the language of the Light among the Night.

Guide me on this path of right.

Let me be the, her thoughts faltered, *Love*

Let me feel the Love.

Let me share the Love.

Illumine-me.

૏૓

Alethea was given a bed in the Gran Mamara's hut. Hut, not house, she learned, as she slowly picked up more and more of what was spoken about her. The only thing she had said in the first few days there was asking for them to not speak to her in Light.

"But I'm supposed to learn it." Juana furrowed her brows at the Gran Mamara.

"There will be plenty of time to learn later," the Gran Mamara admonished. "She wishes to speak Night, then let her. It is hard enough as it is."

Hard enough, was certain. The crutches gave Alethea some leeway when it came to the women. They were clearly set up in groups, with the Gran Mamara leading them. Each day, a different group left at dawn and would come back when the sun was high with the fruits of their hunting. After an afternoon rest, they practiced fighting. The men did much of the cooking and cleaning. There were no gardens though, at least not the kind Alethea was used to. The healing home (home, not hut), where Alethea had been cared for, had a small medicinal garden. It was tended by the poporos.

"There must be something I can do," Alethea said as the Gran Mamara sat with her one afternoon.

The Gran Mamara looked over with a raised eyebrow. Alethea's Night was becoming more fluent, as if she'd just needed a reminder.

"You are our Honored Guest. You are not required to help."

"But there must be something I can do." Alethea watched two men carefully take a woven cloth from a hanging loom.

"What you know how to do is best left for the men." The Gran Mamara harrumphed as she stood and walked away.

Alethea groaned. She watched Tara, Toli's twin sister, come strolling up, a line of three fish on a pole swinging from her back. She plopped them down in front of Alethea.

"I hear Light women know how to do men's tasks," she sneered.

"Tara!" Juana came up behind the girl with a light slap upside the head. "Leave her alone."

Sighing, Alethea struggled up on her crutches. "She's not wrong, though."

Moving from the group, she heard Toli berate Tara for dropping the fish on the wood and not hanging them in the cook hut or giving them directly to him. It was the only thing it seemed the men were allowed to argue about.

A smile crossed her face thinking about Eramaus in this situation, only to be replaced by a pang of heartache. For all she knew, he'd been killed for trying to protect her. Alethea swallowed a sob and hoisted herself into the Gran Mamara's cabana.

The small open hut-like structure had half walls and two chairs. From it, Alethea could see a lot of this town—no, tribal center. It was very different from the towns and villages of the Light. From the cabana, Alethea could see where a waterfall once fell from the caldera of the Holy Mountain. It wasn't flowing. Water was, however, still pooled behind the dam, creating a basin of water beneath the platform before her. After the sun's zenith, the platform would be filled with the women sparring, the clashing of their staves echoing about the center. Behind the platform, an odd mesh of wood and logs and ropes created an agility course the women practiced on. Falling off meant getting wet and starting over.

Was the water still deep enough? Would it ever flow again?

It had stopped the day they attacked the tower.

When mountains steam and streams run dry, you'll know the end of the beginning is nigh, she thought to herself before standing up once more.

Alethea wished she had a tunic like Juana. Instead, she was dressed like Tara: breast band, loin cloth, and a skirt shorter than any Alethea had worn in her youth. She felt exposed and inappropriate. But the tunic was a symbol of status. Juana had one because she was training under the Gran Mamara. Toli also had a tunic, but it didn't peek out from under his breast band. She learned that was because he was training to become a poporo.

Poporos and mamaras, Alethea had figured out, were like psaras and mediki, only reversed. The poporos were all men, but they were the healers and the prayers. The mamaras were all women, they were leaders. Unlike the Light's psaras though, they fought for their positions. The Night had no hierarchy that led up to an emperor. They went from families, to clans, to tribes, to the Gran Mamara.

Alethea made her way back to the Gran Mamara's hut. It was the biggest of all of them and set further 'up-stream' from the others. She threaded her way back across the plank walkways used between the raised platforms, doing her best to ignore the hard stares of the women from their family huts. She could hear the whispers of the men from their cooking huts. There was about one cooking hut to four family huts, and, like Ada Mos's kitchen at home, they were rife with gossip.

The Gran Mamara's hut, however, had a cooking hut to itself. Not that Alethea had seen anyone use it. Normally one of the other men would deliver food for those in her hut to eat. They often stole odd glances at Alethea.

Stopping, Alethea rested by a partially open window. Arguing voices punctured the air, making Alethea swallow. She tried not to listen. She wasn't there to get involved with how the Night led themselves, but it was hard not to when it became obvious Tara was talking about her to the Gran Mamara. Alethea swallowed.

"You ought to leave that burnt demon here. If they want her, then let them have her. We've already done enough."

"Tara!" The Gran Mamara scolded. "You will *NOT* speak of our Honored Guest that way." Her staff pounded on the floor. "Not unless you wish to fight myself *and* Juana at the same time."

There was the sound of someone sitting heavily on the floor. "Why do we even have an *Honored Guest*? Why bring one of those burnt—people—into our midst when they could go back and,"

"Tara," the Gran Mamara cut her off, "it is tradition since the Light's first Lady of Light. Once, during her time as Lady of Light, she joins us at the Gran Fete. I might not have been alive when Lady Katica was here, but I *will* uphold this tradition. Lady Katica took to our way quite well."

"Yeah, well, not like Ah-lee-tia even tries," Tara grumbled.

"Tara!" This time it was Juana who spoke. "She has two broken legs. Even you wouldn't be fighting from two crutches."

"But I'd try."

"And the poporos," the Gran Mamara cut in, "would keep you sleeping to stop you. I do not want to hear another word out of you, or so help me, I'll have Juana leave *you* behind."

Alethea heard the Gran Mamara walk out, her staff thumping on the ground in frustration. She shrunk against the wall until the woman was gone. Letting out her held breath, Alethea was glad she hadn't come her way. Given the woman's mood, she didn't envy those she sparred today.

Chapter 4

Viamas, Alethea learned, was the name of this tribal center, and it had become silent since the Gran Mamara had left with her group three days ago. There had been another quake the day after the Gran Mamara left. Alethea still felt queasy about it. What were the Light doing to displease The Lord even more? But she didn't want to ask the question for fear of what the answer might be. So, she focused on taking Toli's instructions on regaining strength in her legs while Tara and Juana did the hunting and whatever else Night women do.

"Juana!" Tara's voice came with the sound of her feet on the wooden walkways of Viamas.

Juana intercepted her and led her a little way from the hut to speak in quiet tones. Alethea returned to concentrating on her exercises. She was just finishing her set when she noticed Juana pacing before the hut. Sweat trickling down her back, Alethea rose and approached her. Juana stopped to regard Alethea with furrowed brows.

"The Light," she spoke, "have managed to clear a path to the fissure that separates us from them. There have been people working to clear that tall not-tree, the one that collapsed the day you came to us. The Gran Mamara said the tunnel you used led to it."

"I don't think that tunnel is passable," Alethea stated, Night words coming easier to her now. "I, I think it closed behind me. They are," she swallowed, "I think, looking for me, not the tunnel. I don't know if they knew about the tunnel."

Juana nodded and belted out, "TOLI!" over her shoulder.

Toli came at a run, slowing as soon as he saw Alethea standing. She was almost strong enough to only need one crutch. Juana waited for him to join them.

"We need to move, tomorrow."

"Tomorrow?" Toli asked, his eyes widening.

"Yes, tomorrow," Juana confirmed. "I do not want to be here should the Light decide to scour the land for her." She nodded her head to Alethea as she glanced her way. "I suspect you don't either."

"No, I don't," Alethea whispered.

She had little doubt that those working to get access to the Holy Land were not her allies.

Tara piped up from behind her brother, "But the Gran Mamara said—"

"I know the Gran Mamara said we shouldn't leave until she was healed more," Juana glared, "but do you see *us* standing against the Light fighters? Because I do not think they will send them one by one, or even two by two."

"Fine," Tara grumbled.

The rest of the day was spent packing. Toli took care of most of it, while Juana and Tara sparred. Alethea tried to stay out of the way.

Of course it would be raining the next morning. Alethea, who was now great at getting around on the platforms and walkways of Viamas, found being on the uneven ground a much more difficult task. By noon, she wasn't certain if she was soaked in rain or sweat.

"Even the animals know it's better to stay put in this rain," Tara complained as they ate.

"Yes, but I bet even the Light stay inside, right Aletia?"

All the Night had taken to calling Alethea, Aletia. She couldn't recall any th sounds in their language. Aletia, a new name for a new life. A new life? The thought made her crumple inside. No, this wasn't supposed to be a new life, just learning. Yet the despair she felt for all she left behind rose like an ocean wave crashing over her, trying to drown her.

"Aletia?" Toli touched her gently.

She forced a slight smile. "Yes, the Light do not work in the rain."

"Then it is the best time for us to move about. There will be no eyes of Light to see us, nor animals for the watchers to speak with."

"What are the watchers?" Alethea quietly asked Toli as they began to move again.

He looked at her, opened his mouth, then closed it. He tried again and stopped. Then at last uttered, "They are watchers. They watch over their families and the tribal lands, looking for those who don't belong."

"~Guards~?" Alethea used the Light word that she was familiar with.

Toli frowned as he tried to mouth the word. He shrugged.

"~Guards~," Alethea said again before switching to Night. "They move about on the roads, or stand in ~towers~, the tall not-trees, and watch for," she paused. Crime was the word she wanted, but didn't know the translation to Night. "Uh, people doing bad things. But they don't talk to animals."

Juana motioned for silence. Though as the day progressed and the rain got worse, Alethea wasn't sure anyone would have been able to hear them. How Juana knew where she was going, Alethea didn't know. She was now certain it was both sweat *and* rain that soaked her. The rain, unlike her sweat, chilled her to the bone and made stray strands of hair cling to her face. For once, she was thankful for the minimal clothing of the Night. If she had been in a long chiton of the Light, it would have clung to her body and limited her movement.

On the other hand, a braid bun of the Light would have been better in this rain than the two braids she now had. Rivulets ran from their tips down her body, making her shiver. A himation would also be nice. Why didn't the Night have anything similar?

Blinking the thoughts away, Alethea tried to remain alert to her surroundings as a woman of the Night would. She noticed, through the rain fog, a black streak. Juana steered them toward it for a bit before veering to keep them mostly parallel. They stopped as the gray day began to fade into a grayer night. The black smudge was larger now and Alethea couldn't help staring at it.

"The Dark Barrier," Juana spoke.

"Dark Barrier," Alethea repeated before she ate.

"What do the Light call it?" Toli asked, ducking a smack from his twin.

"The ~Dead Zone~," Alethea replied. "Nothing grows on it."

All three of them looked at each other. Tara was the first to laugh. "I don't know what you Burnt Demons do, but things definitely grow in the rocks on this side."

Alethea remembered how the tunnel that she took from The Tower of Light to the Holy Land, was made of that rock. And how the tunnel ended in growth. Tall trees whose roots reached into the soil around the entrance. Were the Light so far from right that they poisoned the ground they walked on? But why only near the Dead Zone?

A barrier erected to keep the peace, the wind whispered, *but a barrier maintained when peace was not so close to being had.*

And for a moment, Alethea saw people fighting. People who looked both Light and Dark, where only their clothing marked them apart. And the Night won their mountains and the Light retreated to the sea. She blinked and the image was gone.

₦)CR

There would be no getting dry, apparently, as they had slept wet despite the large wide leaves of the gingko tree blocking much of the rain. Today it continued its assault as they drew nearer the Dead Zone, no, Dark Barrier.

"There's no way she'll be able to cross without getting caught," Tara complained as she thumbed back at Alethea. "She's too slow; two days for a one day journey?"

If Juana responded, Alethea didn't hear. They had made it to the Dark Barrier now and walked along it. Plants really did grow there, some draping down as if to reach for the Light. They stopped at a gaping maw that went into it.

"She's never going to get down on those things," Tara whined.

Juana sighed. "Tara, why don't you and Toli go down and get the casita ready for us. I'll make sure Aletia gets there, all right?"

Tara huffed and started down. "Keep up Toli," she called back.

Toli gave a pleading glance at Juana, who urged him onward. With a heavy sigh, he followed his twin. Alethea felt a tinge of sorrow for him. He was so sweet and kind, such an opposite to her. Juana stood by the cave entrance listening and watching.

"Sadly, there is no tunnel that goes all the way between here and our land over there," Juana gestured out across to where Alethea was sure the three peaks would have been visible on a clear day. "But we have a casita at the bottom of the tunnel, so we can wait until the time is right."

Juana stepped into the cave and beckoned Alethea forward. At first the floor was easy, but darkness soon enveloped them. Alethea felt her ankle move awkwardly and stifled a cry.

"Stay there," Juana told her. "There should be, hah!" There was the sound of something scraping, then a light flared into existence. "Did you not use a torch in your tunnel?"

"Um, no, it was, um, lit by, ~faith~?"

Alethea wasn't sure she wanted to mention the bones of the people that lit as she had walked by them. Sure, Lady Bronte's diary had said they'd given their lives willingly, but that didn't mean it wasn't unsettling. Juana shrugged, not questioning her uncertainty.

They took their time moving down the tunnel. Sometimes Alethea used the walls for a crutch, sometimes she used Juana. There were a few points where Juana had to help her down a very steep part. By the time Alethea had squeezed herself into the cave at the bottom she was ready to sleep. Juana led her to a bed.

"Took long enough," Tara harrumphed.

"And you will be the first person I challenge at the Gran Fete if you keep this up," Juana barked at her.

"I could take you."

Before Alethea could blink, Juana's staff was pointed at the girl's throat, Tara's hand only halfway to her own. "Tara, you *will* cut it out or I *will* be sure you are marked as dishonorable."

Tara's hand went back into her lap. Her face fell into a deep scowl and she turned away from them. Juana pulled her staff back and went to her own bed. Toli quietly served them food. Alethea desperately wanted to know what being marked dishonorable meant. The way Juana said it made it sound like a real punishment. But neither Toli nor Juana were close enough for her to ask, and sleep took over quickly.

$\mathcal{SO}\mathcal{CR}$

Dreams came and went in the night. Alethea woke as she heard movement about her. Her legs ached from yesterday, dully throbbing. She tried to picture what the map looked like for this part of the land, but she'd never studied maps before, merely glanced at them. Toli was already making breakfast and Juana was whispering heatedly with Tara from the casita entrance. Tara occasionally made a gesture at her, but Alethea couldn't seem to will her body up.

"Fine, go find meat, but don't go far and *do NOT* take from the Light," Juana said loud enough for Alethea to hear.

Tara's reply was muttered, but it earned her a smack upside the head. Juana stayed in the doorway for a moment, watching Tara retreat into the gray mist, before she turned around and caught Alethea's eyes.

"How are you feeling?"

"You should just leave me here with supplies," Alethea responded.

Juana chuckled. "Don't listen to Tara, she's full of pessimism. Take today to recover. You did well these last two days."

She turned to Toli, her back now to Alethea. But Alethea noticed Toli's furtive glances in her direction and the shake of his head. She was slowing them down. Whatever this Gran Fete was, it seemed they would rather be there than here with her. And, if she remembered correctly, it was only held every twelve years. Even Juana would have been a child at the last one.

Alethea lay back down and closed her eyes. She was just a burden right now. How could she learn the ways of the Night if she couldn't even walk well, let alone fight? No. She couldn't let it be this way. She had a promise to keep to The Lord. And if she kept *her* promise, then he'd better be keeping *His* to her.

Sitting up, Alethea spoke aloud in Light for the first time

since she'd joined the Night. "~Lord of Light!~" She ignored that above her was rock, reaching instead for the light from the entrance. "~Heal me that I may follow this path you lay before me. Let me walk again and become whole. Illumine-*Me!*~"

Light poured in through the gray, filling her hands. She poured it onto her legs, vaguely aware Juana and Toli had rushed toward her. She caught Toli stopping Juana from coming closer. The more the light poured out, the fainter she felt, but the better her legs were. When she could hold herself up no more, her hands collapsed to her knees and she lay back, her vision slowly eclipsing into darkness.

Alethea wasn't sure how long she was out, but when she awoke, Toli was examining her legs. Alethea shifted, and Juana looked at her and immediately offered her food.

"Eat."

There was no arguing the tone, nor Alethea's stomach. So, she ate. As soon as she was done, Toli had her lie down as he checked the mobility of her legs. He kept glancing at her as if expecting her to wince in pain.

"How'd you do that? Can you teach me?"

"You better not learn Burnt Magic," Tara growled from where she sat, as far from Alethea as she could.

Alethea felt her face flush. "I don't know, I just pray, and The Lord listens. I don't know if your Lady would do the same."

The wind laughed around her. *We will for you and might for him, but few are worthy*, the female voice whispered.

"But just think, if we could heal like that, none of the warriors would have to stay in the Healing Home for long. And we—"

He was cut short by a look from Juana.

"I guess we know why the Light never seem to die from our arrows, if they can be healed like that," came Tara's bitter reply.

"No," Alethea responded, "I, have been gifted with this ability. I don't think there are many,"—

Only the chosen few, the wind confirmed,—"who can," Alethea finished.

"The Lady of Night would never concede to give out power like your Lord of Light," Tara spat.

Alethea sighed as she studied the girl, so full of vitriol.

"Tara," she spoke softly as Toli handed her more food. "It is not our Gods, The Lord of Light and The Lady of Night who hate each other. It is us, the people, who hate. It is a divide between us like the Dark Barrier. Love is what we should embrace, not hate."

Tara just snorted and turned to face the wall. She stayed like that for the rest of the evening.

Juana sat by Alethea to eat. "I'm sorry, she," Juana tried to formulate words for her apology.

"Don't," Alethea shook her head. "Like the Light, not all Night are going to like me."

It was, Alethea thought, just a fact of her life. She'd seen it in the Light, and it made sense to see it in the Night as well. After all, she was a bit of each. Wasn't that why she was chosen? And she would need to work with it, and around it. She was certain there was no time to make friends with those who wouldn't return her friendship.

Chapter 5

Rain, of course, had to pour down on Eramaus and the two remaining prisoners, neither of whom, he was certain, were Bleeding Hearts. Eramaus wasn't sure what happened to the others, just that they had been taken out a few days ago and had not come back.

"Fourteen bodies," the one grumbled. "How many were sent in against a helpless old woman?"

Eramaus pushed his hair from his eyes and looked at the man. "Thea Lady wasn't old, and she could call on The Lord to protect herself."

The man blinked at him. "You saying the old bat had a successor?"

"Lady Katica wasn't an old bat." Eramaus stopped working to glare at the man.

The man's companion whispered something in his ear. Whatever it was, he didn't say anything else as the whip cracked, forcing them back to work.

For what it was worth, twenty-five days of hard labor had found them at the base of the tower. There had been no level below that anything had fallen into. They hadn't created any pit, they were just at ground level. The only spot left was next to the Dead Zone. No one wanted to touch it. Eramaus knew they should clear it, but he couldn't bring himself to do it. How would he be able to stand finding Alethea's mutilated corpse?

He looked toward Emelye just in time to see Darian exchanging words with her. If the herbs he'd given his cousin didn't seem to actually work, Eramaus would have just attacked him rather than finish that corner. When Darian glanced his way, his index finger curled to his thumb in the symbol of the Bleeding Hearts. Eramaus glared. *Be helpful, he thought, but do not claim to be one of them if you are not laboring with us.* Darian hurried away.

At lunch, Emelye managed to whisper to him what Darian had told her.

"High Psara Perroa arrived two days ago. He was questioned privately by Poulos, as were all the High Psara. He still remains in good standing."

"And why should I care about that?" Eramaus grumbled.

"Because Perroa is trying to get us released—"

Emelye stopped as the bold figure of the Paladin strode toward him. She deftly covered their talk as if she had just handed Eramaus his food. Of course, the man would stop before him. Eramaus took a bite, chewing as rudely as he could.

Poulos smirked. "You best apply yourself to clearing the wall near the Dead Zone. Don't think I haven't noticed you avoiding it." A flash of horror must have crossed Eramaus's face for the Paladin laughed. "Ah yes, I do think that *is* where we will find the false Lady's body."

Eramaus gulped down his bite as the Paladin turned and walked away. But as much as he wanted to retort, to say something, words failed him. The other two prisoners clearing away ruble watched as he glumly walked to his assigned corner. He stared at it until rain blurred his vision and the whip cracked across his back.

He moved slowly. Taking deep breaths, trying to prepare himself for what he might see. It wasn't like he hadn't seen Thea nearly dead before, but, but he'd saved her both times. What good would it be to save her now? It was not as if they could just fly away like the Night could. So, he refused to move any faster than his snail's pace, though the whip stung more than once.

Finally, the others were made to join him, and together they pried out a large rock. As it fell forward, they all jumped back. Rubble tumbled down with it and they all stared.

"That, that's not right, is it?" The man from before spoke.

"No," Eramaus responded.

Solid black rock filled what looked like a doorway, radiating warmth. It was as if the Dead Zone had liquefied to fill the space. But worse than that, and what they all stared at, was the charred body half in and half out of it.

Eramaus swallowed. Please don't let that be Thea, he thought. The whip cracked. But none of them moved or spoke. Finally, on the third crack, Eramaus found his voice.

"Call Poulos back!"

As he stared at the body, trying to decipher if it was Alethea, a burst of sun split the clouds, hitting the corpse. For a moment, Eramaus's heart leapt. It couldn't be Thea. And then it fell.

He knew that tattoo. Kadmus, Captain Boreas's nephew, had no qualms showing it to everyone. And Kadmus was known to be rough on women. If he was there, then Alethea was ahead of him, which meant...

She was encased in black rock.

Dead.

Eramaus howled into the rain.

❦

The moment the Paladin laid eyes on the last body, he ordered the prisoners to be taken to their cells. The rain shifted to a drizzle by morning, its gray mood suiting Eramaus's. He traced figures in the dirt of his cell floor. Images of Alethea screaming as she was enveloped in that warm black rock plagued his mind. He wished Darian had brought them herbs that could dull his brain, let him sleep and think no more of the horror he was living. All those bodies, all fifteen of them, alive or dead, those men had been sent in to capture her.

Knowing Kadmus had been there revolted him. He'd seen how that man had looked at Thea back when this, this hellacious journey began. He knew of that man's appetite. He hoped he suffered more than Alethea from that black rock. He hoped The Lord had a special place for Kadmus in the coldest of afterlives.

Eramaus's thoughts were cut short by the sound of marching echoing toward them. He moved to his cell door. Had Alethea been trapped in a pocket surrounded by the rock? Had they found her and were taking her to a cell? But there was no way. No way Thea had survived. It had been over sixteen days since the last man alive was found.

Eramaus brought his thoughts to the present, as bleak as the present was. He watched as Knight Sendhil stopped in Emelye's cell. He couldn't hear what was said to her, though her response was clear.

"She wasn't a false Lady and you know it."

Knight Sendhil's sigh was deep.

"Em," Eramaus pleaded, suddenly realizing it was her chance for freedom.

Everyone turned to him. Eramaus swallowed. He tried to speak, tried to denounce Thea as Lady of Light, but, she was—

in his mind, in his heart—even if she might not be alive. Grief tried to choke him and he heard Emelye sigh in the silence.

"Lady Katica thought she was to be the next Lady of Light," Emelye stated. "Lady Katica thought that we should protect her Light, so in honor of Lady Katica, we defended her."

Knight Sendhil turned to her and nodded. He then turned to Eramaus.

"What she said," he forced himself to say, trying desperately not to cry.

The man nodded again and spoke quietly to his group. Three men pivoted and came to Eramaus's door. They opened it and he was brought before the Knight. This close to the man, Eramaus could see how haggard he was. It was as if he'd been up more nights than he'd slept. The Knight returned Eramaus's gaze.

"It is a break in tradition," the knight shook his head, "but I must do as the Paladin orders."

Eramaus tried to read the man's expression. Tried to gauge if it meant Eramaus and Emelye were about to walk out of there free, or to be hung as traitors. Two of the squires took him each by an arm. Don't resist, he reminded himself as his body twitched despite his exhaustion.

"Squire Eramaus, formerly the fifth son of Drakon Spanos, Duke of Gorgomilos and his wife, Stephana Vasil," the man intoned, "you are hereby stripped of all rank, including that of squire, and banished from Holy City of Archtheos and may not return to the Capital City of Paramythia unless it be with a man of good standing who will vouch for your behavior."

Eramaus glanced to his cousin. She rubbed her wrist where a criminal's bracelet lay against her skin. The armorer now faced him.

"Present your right wrist." Sendhil intoned, remaining expressionless.

Eramaus yearned to know what the knight thought. Was he for or against Thea? The man cleared his throat. Swallowing, Eramaus presented his wrist. Being marked this way meant they were to leave here alive. But to what end? Why give him this freedom when all he hoped for was dead. He ignored the warm wind that tried to whisper reassurances in his ear. Listening to The Lord only caused him pain.

"By the power of The Lord and Emperor," Sendhil clamped the bracelet around Eramaus's wrist, "you are hereby marked as a criminal and shall be deemed suitable for menial labor only." He locked the bracelet together and pulled two flaming straws from a torch. "Illuminus," he spoke as he touched one flame to the hinge while thrusting the other inside the lock.

Eramaus hissed at the heat of the flames as they melted the soft metal, sealing the bracelet shut. Prayers like that shouldn't be answered, he thought. How could The Lord answer these prayers while trying to whisper to him that it would be all right? Eramaus scowled.

Another squire handed him a coarse kolobus.

"Change and return your squire robes," Knight Sendhil commanded.

Eramaus complied, not that his squire robes were worth much after all the excavation he'd done. The three knights behind him moved him forward so that he now marched behind Emelye. His cousin had been stripped of her mediki robes, now wearing a chiton that barely fit.

"Waste of a good soldier, too," Eramaus heard Sendhil mutter as he passed them to lead the procession.

They walked out into a light drizzle and marched through the streets to the gates of Paramythia. Few people stopped to look at the procession as they kept their heads covered by their himations or chlamys. Maybe there wouldn't be anyone to throw stones at them when the guards left, like he'd seen done in Gorgomilos when he was eight. Eramaus swallowed the memory with the bile that rose in his throat.

Rivulets of rain running down their faces, they stopped just outside the gates to Paramythia. Sendhil gave a soft order to his squires, and one by one they all nodded and filed away. Sendhil stood alone with Eramaus and Emelye, staring off into the haze of the rain.

Eramaus placed a hand on Emelye's shoulder to guide her away. The further they were from the wall, the better it would be.

"I am sorry." The Knight's voice made Eramaus turn back to the man. His face was filled with sorrow, and he looked back to Eramaus. "Too much tradition has been broken, it's no wonder The Lord of Light is angry with us." And with that, he turned from them.

"Wait," Eramaus called to him.

The man looked over his shoulder.

"Can you tell me what day it is?"

"The twenty-sixth day," he called back as he walked away, "of the second month in the year of Our Lord eight hundred and forty-one."

Emelye shivered. They didn't even have a single chlamys between them to keep the rain off.

"Walk," Eramaus started forward, "and pray someone won't decide it'd be fun to kill us."

"You are such a ball of sunshine, cousin," Emelye retorted.

Putting one foot before the other, Eramaus left the place he'd begun to call home, where Alethea's body lay under ruins. Tears mingled with the rain on his cheeks.

⁂

"Eramaus?"

Emelye's voice broke his zone just as he'd managed to blank his mind. He scrunched his nose and growled slightly.

She sighed. "I'm sure it will be all right."

Stopping, he turned to face her. "All right? All right? Did you not see the tower fall?" He gestured wildly to where it should have been visible.

"Yes, but *I* wasn't the one laughing like a maniac when it did so." Her hands went to her hips as she stared up into his face. She dared step closer. "So why *were* you laughing when the tower fell? Did The Lord tell you she would survive?"

"No, Emelye. Even if I trusted what The Lord says, it's never clear and never helpful in *any* way. Has *He* told *you* something useful?"

"No," Emelye snorted at him. "All *I* get is dead silence."

"Just like Thea," he muttered, pivoting and walking a little faster.

"You think she's dead."

Emelye's tone was hard to read. Not that he wanted to read it anyway. She could be mad, she could be sympathetic, he really didn't care. He'd thought his heart had broken when Thea pledged herself to be The Lord's bride. This, this emptiness, this pain—this was a broken heart. And it would never mend.

Ever.

Emelye caught up and placed a hand on his arm. "Think about it, Eramaus."

"About Thea's death? I can't *not* think about it. I dream of it, and all the times I've failed her. And—"

"Eramaus," Emelye's tone scolded slightly, and he paused enough to glance at her. "Why would The Lord let her die *now*," she continued, "when he's ensured she was saved so many times before?"

"But *I* couldn't save her, Em. My body went limp before I could get there."

"And how do you think she got to the Holy Land without using the Pilgrim's Path?"

"I don't." But Eramaus stopped, remembering how he'd watch for her to cross the top of the Tower before going up the Pilgrim's Path, to listen for the conch shell to sound. For a moment, hope flickered inside, until recollection hit him. "She didn't cross the top of the Tower, Em. She'd always cross the tower before going to the Holy Land. And there was that hot black rock. It encased Kadmus, and—"

"Move aside, peasant! Caravan coming through." A man cracked his whip.

Eramaus instinctually placed himself between Em and the road. The man cracked his whip again, forcing Eramaus and Emelye against the fence that lined the roadway. Looking at the canvas covering the wagons, Eramaus blinked. The date Sendhil had stated clicked in his head. Captain Boreas was nothing but consistent with Count Manella's supply wagons. And, if he wasn't mistaken, that was Count Manella's signet on those wagons. A tiny glimmer of hope bloomed, only to quickly fade once more.

What was the point? Boreas was going into Paramythia. They needed a sponsor to vouch for them to get in. He sighed and began to walk opposite the caravan's direction, keeping his arms crossed over the bracelet, trying his best to look like a poor pilgrim returning home from his pilgrimage. No need for him to be laughed at by the men he'd once been a part of. How many more bridges would he burn?

"Eramaus," Emelye hissed at him as she began to follow.

"Just, keep your head down and bracelet covered."

His stomach rumbled, echoed by hers. Lord, were they going to need to beg? He didn't have long to contemplate that, when one of the men shoved them off the road. He laughed as Eramaus stumbled into Emelye, making her fall against the fence.

"Hey!" The familiar voice of Captain Boreas spoke as a pony's hooves beat on the ground, coming up to them. "I swear, if you do not control your urges, I will leave you in the pass and the Night can do with you what they will."

"Shadow slaves," the man grumbled.

Eramaus dared glance at the Captain before quickly helping Emelye. He knew the Captain's hard stare and he knew the man it was aimed at. Too bad that man hadn't gone with Kadmus to attack the Tower and die.

"I'm fine." Emelye glared at the man's back as he hurriedly marched forward.

There was a soft thud as Captain Boreas dismounted. "Are ye, though?"

Eramaus raised his eyes, unable to keep himself from fidgeting with the bracelet that now graced his wrist. The Captain's rough hand came to his shoulder. Eramaus said nothing, though he wanted to say everything.

"I heard what happened," the Captain spoke quietly. "Come, ride in the back wagon. I feel there is much to discuss."

"But," Emelye began to protest, stopping at the Captain's sad smile.

"I see what ye hide. But don't ye worry, Lass. I know the way things work. Ye be needing a man of good standing, and few are better than I." He winked.

Emelye opened her mouth to speak, but Eramaus shook his head. The last of the wagons was passing, and Boreas turned from them to re-mount his pony. He made a couple of hand gestures to the rear guard before riding up to the driver of the last wagon. Eramaus knew these two, Basil and Giles. They were good men, and he urged Emelye forward as Basil beckoned them to the wagon as it slowed.

"Do I dare ask," Basil whispered to Eramaus as he showed them the compartment under the sacks of goods, "what got you from honored squire to exiled criminal?"

Emelye snorted. "We supported the wrong side apparently."

"Well not everyone can see the light in the dark."

He curled his thumb around his pointer, the other three fingers up, and placed his hand on his heart. He winked as he closed Eramaus and Emelye into darkness.

❧❦

Eramaus and Emelye remained hidden until Captain Boreas brought them dinner, late. Basil and Giles accompanied him, and the Captain told Eramaus and Em not to trust any but him and them. Eramaus remembered them vaguely from his time as a mercenary with Boreas. And here he was, instructed to stay in the loft above the stable of the Pokemoke Inn. How funny it was to be back in the place he'd gone the night Alethea had been stabbed.

Stabbed.

Trying not to curl in on himself as if he'd been dealt that blow, Eramaus turned from the others. He climbed up the ladder wishing he could leave, or at least get a drink. How could they talk and converse like that with Thea gone? Didn't they know how pointless it all was? What were they supposed to be protecting without her? He couldn't even carry out her last request and protect Prince Lyrcus.

Eramaus punched the beam nearest him, immediately regretting it. He nursed his skinned knuckles, flopping into the hay to stare morosely at the ceiling.

"Eramaus," the Captain spoke from the top of the ladder.

Eramaus ignored him.

"Lad, I know this t'ain't easy for ye." The man was closer now, and Eramaus turned away. "But there is—"

"Nothing," Eramaus completed. "She's gone. Dead. I should be too. There's nothing left."

"Oh, Lad." Heaving a sigh, the Captain placed a kind hand on Eramaus's shoulder. "Would that the world worked differently. But ye understand, the Bleeding Hearts, we ain't just fer her. We're for all the people who has light like hers who are in danger of it being snuffed."

"Like there could be people with light like Thea Lady's. She outshone them all." The past tense tasted like blood in his mouth.

"Aye, I won't disagree with ya there. But tell me, would ye have yer cousin Emelye's light snuffed out? Or that of Darian's?"

"Darian is a traitor." Eramaus finally turned to the Captain. "He *confessed* to having been led astray so he wouldn't be imprisoned with Emelye and me. Given Lady Thea named *him* as one she trusted, he should—"

"Eramaus." The Captain's firm tone stopped his flow of words. The man's grin tightened. "You listen, and you listen well. Darian *confessed* so we would still have a man on the inside. Emelye should have done the same, but—"

"She fell for Thea Lady, same as I did," Eramaus finished softly.

The Captain blinked and chuckled as his grip loosened. "Well, tha would explain how her fire is tha same as yours. Cousin, she said she was, from which side?"

"My mother's," Eramaus grumbled, crossing his arms.

The Captain nodded. "We'll see that you get a chance to speak with your mother. For now, lay low." He let go of Eramaus. "And be nice to your cousin. She's got light too, even if it be at a fraction of what Alethea's is."

"Was," Eramaus muttered, stalking away before the Captain could say anything else.

Chapter 6

Tara and Juana led them through the fields, each one of them remaining in the cultivated rows of tall plants. Alethea wasn't sure what it was, some sort of grain. She sighed as Tara glanced back at her with a smirk. She hurried forward a bit to be in step with Toli, though there was grain between them.

"Aletia," Toli spoke softly.

Alethea glanced at him.

"Why didn't you heal yourself like that before?"

"Well, I," Alethea paused, thinking through her answer. "Healing like that takes strength. And, um, it would not be nice to heal myself when the poporos cared for me even though I am not Night."

"Then will you go back to your people after the Gran Fete?" Toli asked. "I know the tribe of the big place hates you, but surely there's another tribe or clan that will take you? Everyone has a clan."

Alethea glanced at Toli, his young face so innocent. How did she explain the politics of the Light that she barely understood when she wasn't even certain of the politics of the

Night?

"It's," she paused trying to figure out the right words. "The tribe of the big place is like your tribe of Viamas. All other tribes, and thus clans, follow them." She paused again, thinking how to phrase what she wanted to say. "There are, families, that do not hate me, but," she glanced toward the lightening sky, "The Lord of Light, and I think your Lady of Night, have tasked me to bring our peoples together. And I cannot find the Night who are willing if I do not stay with them."

Toli gasped, and she stopped as he reached through the grain to touch her. He gazed at her in wide-eyed wonder.

"When you follow the chosen into the sun," he spoke quietly exuberant, "know that our peoples will now be one." He took in an excited breath. "Are you, are you the chosen one?"

Alethea blinked. "The Night have a prophecy on becoming one with the Light?"

Toli nodded. He leaned in, as if not wanting the others to hear, though they were far ahead now. "When a child of the Night becomes Lady of Light, old wounds she'll heal and try to make right. But when the lakes steam and the waters run dry, the end of the beginning is nigh. When you follow the chosen into the sun, know that our peoples will now be one."

Alethea swallowed. She should have known. It would make sense if both sides were to unite, there would be a prophecy for each. She motioned them forward so they could catch up to the others before Tara complained, again.

"It's so similar," she told him, "to the one Lady Katica told me." She fumbled her way through translating it to Night. "When mountains steam, and springs run dry, know that the end of beginning is nigh. Take heart, those who have no doubt, one will be chosen to lead you out. Beware those who have no belief, for a broken land, you will not leave. Heed the child of the Night, blessed by the Light, for she will guide you as our

Gods reunite."

ॐ

The further from the Dark Barrier they went, the slower Tara became. They crossed a few fences, though there were no houses nearby. Each time they came to one, Tara stopped to glance about before beckoning them on. At the last fence, she had them crouch low. The grass inside it was shorter, and they followed it as it pointed them toward the mountains rising before them.

"We should have left last night," she hissed at Juana as the fence turned and they had to cross it.

"Aletia needed rest, and you know there is no casita on the other side," Juana hissed back. "We will be fine."

"And there is always someone on the wide path at this time," Tara grumbled.

Alethea wasn't certain who would be on the road at this early hour. There weren't any dwellings nearby, though she could see the smoke curling from a single chimney in the distance. A crowing rooster made them all pause, but Tara urged them onward toward the line of trees in the distance. The closer they got, the more hunkered down they got, till at last they were almost crawling through the tall grasses beside a road.

"I don't like this." Tara looked up and down the road before fixing her sight to the south.

Alethea looked that way too. A spec in the distance was coming closer. There was no way to tell how far away it was, though she was certain the person was riding a pony.

"Cross now, and get down once you're on the other side," Juana hissed. "GO!"

Juana shoved Tara, who stumbled then quickly ran over to the other side, diving into the cover of a bush. Juana sent Toli next, who quickly scrambled up into the high branches of the tree. Juana grabbed Alethea's arm, and, keeping them crouched low, hurried them both across. Juana swung up into the tree, but Alethea laid flat, hoping the grasses would cover her.

She could hear the hooves now. Breathing to its steady rhythm, she dared look up as the sound came nearer. For a moment, her breathing stopped. But the pony maintained its speed, the rider focused on where he was going. His kolobus was stained with mud kicked up from the pony's hooves. His chlamys flapped about him as it worked its way off his body. Turning his head, he reached out to catch it before it fluttered away. Alethea froze as his eyes gazed across her.

"Hiya!" His heals spurred his pony on, head snapping back to the road.

"You let him see you," Tara hissed.

"I didn't mean to be seen," Alethea whispered.

"Yes, well now they may go hunting for you up in Damadiosa. Is that what you want?"

Alethea blinked, she didn't even know where Damadiosa was, let alone how to get to it.

"Tara," Juana's voice cut the silence. "That is enough! I doubt that man holds enough rank to do anything. Right, Aletia?"

"No." Alethea shook her head. At least she hadn't seen any of the colors that might mark him as a servant to The Lord or Emperor. Then again, she hadn't been looking.

Lord of Light, Lady of Night she thought as they continued on, *Keep my friends safe, both new and old, and let our journeys be in peace. Illumine and enlighten us.*

⛄

The further from the road they went, the more relaxed the others became. It wasn't long before the Dark Barrier loomed high above them. Alethea and Toli were told to stay put as Tara and Juana scouted for the passage up.

"All *her* fault we didn't aim right," Tara grumbled as she went her way, ignoring Juana's glare.

Toli bounced eagerly on the balls of his feet. He kept looking to Alethea like he wanted to spill his words out but didn't know where to start. Before he sorted himself out, a bird call came from Juana's direction.

"She found it!" Toli cried, and bounded off before slowing down so Alethea could keep up.

Tara passed them not long after, sneering at Alethea as she went by. She dragged her brother with her, despite his protests. Alethea wouldn't put it past the girl to run up whatever tunnel they were going into next without her. But she hadn't, for she was roped to Juana, who was roped to Toli. Juana added Alethea after Toli as Tara stared into a jagged crevasse.

Each step took them further into darkness, and before long, Alethea might as well have been blind. There was a strange softness to the floor. It squished like mud between her toes, and she didn't like it.

"Are, are we not going to use a torch to light our way?" Alethea whispered as she stumbled into Toli for a third time as the path zigzagged upwards.

"Not yet," he whispered. "You don't want to disturb the bats."

She looked back but saw nothing. She wanted to pray to glow, but decided perhaps disturbing the bats might not be a good idea. But the darkness hurt, her eyes straining to find any bit of light to see by. She gave up and closed them, only to bump into Toli as they stopped.

Toli reached back and took her hand as they began to move forward again. Move, stop, move stop. Toli squeezed her hand for each stop and start so she would not bump into him.

Hours later, the darkness was pierced by the sound of

running water. When they were nearly upon it, they stopped for the longest pause yet.

Long pause, short move, another long pause, then short move, long pause. In each pause, the water sounded interrupted. As she could feel the water, Toli spoke.

"Move forward to where the water is. Be careful of your step and wash your feet."

"Wash my feet?" she asked as she stepped forward to the water.

"Yes, there's water that flows from one level to another. Let it run over your feet for a bit. Don't touch your feet, or you could get sick."

"All right." Alethea nodded. Not that he could see her nod.

She let go of Toli's hand to feel for the stream of water. It was narrow and tumbled down the uneven wall. Stepping toward it, Alethea felt her foot sink into nothing, and she pushed herself back. There was no pool, just an opening to below. Taking a breath, she balanced herself against the wall and let her foot be washed over. Then she did the same with the other.

"Done," she whispered.

They continued on. The floors here didn't have that same squishy mud on it. Alethea wondered if they were ever going to light anything. She decided to keep her eyes closed until they did.

"That's not supposed to be there." Tara's voice made her open her eyes.

A tiny bit of light filtered through a crack in the ceiling. To Alethea, it felt like a small beacon of hope.

"No one left us a torch either." Juana felt along a far wall.

"Maybe I can?" Alethea looked up at the crevice as they looked to her. She reached her hand up, silently praying. *Lord of Light, Lady of Night, let me bring a bit of light to illuminate and enlighten us in the dark.*

Sure enough, she could feel the light pooling in her hand, heard the gasp of the others, felt the jerk on the rope.

"Burnt Demon sorcery. I want no part of it," Tara hissed.

"And how are you going to climb if you can't see the next hand hold?" Juana queried.

"I can climb this path blind," Tara retorted.

"Sure, but if there is a crevice here, when there was not one before, might not the climbing path be different?" Juana countered.

Alethea used her other hand to close off the pooling light. She didn't want a lot of it, just enough to provide them with some sight. Bringing her hands to her chest, she cupped the tiny ball. She looked between her companions. Tara looked disgusted, Juana showed no emotion, but Toli gazed curiously at the light.

"Can I touch it?" he looked up to her.

"No." Tara grabbed him and pulled him back.

"Tara, don't be an idiot. A little bit of gathered sunlight isn't going to hurt you."

Alethea played with the ball in her hand, very uncertain of what to do with it, till at last she tossed it up. "Illumine and Enlighten our path."

The light spread out before them, diffusing from its ball form to be a soft cloud lighting their way from the cave. Even Tara gasped as it illuminated a pit of blackness. Most of the glow was up where Juana stood. It undulated like an impatient child being made to wait.

"Would you rather be in the back, with Aletia in the front, so you can be as far as possible from the light."

"No," Tara grumbled as she led them forward.

The path became steeper and steeper as they went, until it was near vertical. They picked their way carefully up, a hand-hold here, a foothold there. Twice Alethea lost her grip, nearly taking Toli down, if it hadn't been for Juana's strong arm catching her.

By the time they reached the top and collapsed on the ground, it was dusk.

"We'll camp here," Juana told them.

Alethea dismissed her light, only too happy to lie down and sleep.

Chapter 7

∾∾

They stayed in the tavern for another day and a half. Well, Eramaus stayed in the hay loft. He didn't know what Emelye did when she left the loft. Though she was always bringing him food and drink. Not that he ate enough for her liking. She had the audacity to compare his eating habits to Thea's.

Thea.

His heart ached. If only he'd stayed in the tower instead of leaving with Prince Lyrcus. Then he could have died defending her. What was the point of living if she wasn't around.

Emelye sat down on day two with lunch. He could feel her staring at him, though he looked at the wall, ignoring the food.

"They haven't found her," Emelye told him.

"She's buried in the hot rock," Eramaus countered.

"No sign of that being the case," Emelye cheerily continued. "And though Poulos has tried to chip it away, so far they've just managed to burn some prisoner's feet off. Glad it wasn't you."

Eramaus turned to look at his cousin. "You really believe she survived?"

"Yes." She met his gaze. "You don't have to save her every time, you know. When Lowri tried, and I mean *tried*, to poison her, she found a way to counter it." Emelye chewed a bit, thoughtfully. "And taking into account that she got to the Holy Land without using the path everyone else took, I'd like to think she did it then too. And I'm not the only one."

Eramaus studied his cousin as she chewed her food. She pushed the plate of it toward him and he took some.

"Okay, but how is she surviving up there? Could *you* survive in the wilderness on *your* own? Cause I'm not sure Thea was ever taught to cook, let alone catch dinner."

He chomped down on the bread, chewing aggressively as he watched Emelye. Her face fell, but only for a moment.

"I bet she's made friends." Emelye nodded as if that solved everything.

Eramaus looked at her incredulously. "Do you really think the Night would take her? Do you think she looks enough like one of them, too?"

"All I'm saying is that I bet she can blend in with both sides. And she'd make friends with the Night,"

"Thea was all LIGHT!" he interrupted, grabbing cheese and storming off to another part of the loft.

He grabbed onto a rafter as the building shook.

"Eramaus!" Fear caught in Emelye's voice.

Eramaus swung over, catching her arm, swinging her toward him. They clung to a beam as the hay shifted. Ponies stomped at their stall doors, neighing in fear. Somewhere outside, people screamed. Eramaus held tight to the beam as he held tight to his cousin. The building tilted, their food scattering below. And then silence as things stopped. Someone wailed.

"We need to get out of here," Eramaus looked at the dangerous tilt to the walls.

"How?" Emelye looked at him. "We can't go around with

these foul bracelets on." She shook hers at him. "As it is, all I'm doing is playing scullery maid to make sure we get food while Captain Boreas tries to get the documentation we need."

Eramaus looked at the bracelets. He held his arm out next to Emelye's. The ground trembled again, but only the loosest of things shifted. He grabbed Emelye's right hand with his right hand.

"Lord of Light," he looked to the ceiling, "if you still have things for Em and I to do, release the bands from our wrists, that we may do them better. Illuminus!"

"Eramaus, I don't think,"

But before Emelye could finish, the bracelets glowed. They warmed to near burning before breaking apart and falling to the floor. Eramaus let go of Emelye's hand.

There is indeed still much for you to do, the wind whispered, ruffling his hair. *For those who rule are truly the fool.*

Great, you answer my prayer, but what about my questions?

But the presence was gone. Heaving a sigh, Eramaus encouraged Emelye to follow him. He made sure the ladder was steady enough to climb down before beginning his descent.

"Apparently," he snorted, "The Lord of Light's had it with our ruling fools."

ॐ

Alethea was glad they hadn't gone far from the Dark Barrier for their rest. But when they woke, Tara was gone. At first it didn't feel unusual. Tara liked to hunt first thing, but she wasn't back by the time they had packed camp. Juana looked to Toli, who shrugged.

"She's not hurt. I'd feel that." He sighed.

"And she told you nothing of where she was going?" Juana sounded worried.

"It's been years since we had that kind of connection." Toli sighed again. "Ever since –" he stopped.

"The Gran Mamara, "Juana continued, "encouraged you to become a poporo, I know." She patted his shoulder. "Go see if Tara's with your mother in Damadiosa. Talk with the Gran Mamara, tell her what's happened. Meet us at the last bridge and let us know what she says."

There was pain mixed with fear in Toli's eyes. "Maybe you should go."

Juana shook her head. "Tara won't hurt you. The path is safe for you." She turned to Alethea, "Aletia, climb that tree and stay in the upper branches. Don't move until I get back."

"I –" Alethea paused, looking between the two of them. Their concern was palpable.

"Toli, go," Juana shooed him off and he scurried away. She turned back to Alethea. "Their mother tends to hang with the banished crowd, her cousin, Brisa, in particular. That's why their matriarch sent Tara to Viamas with Toli."

"And Brisa is bad?"

Juana nodded. "She nearly started a war when she was in Viamas. Hates Light with a burning passion. Claims they violated and killed her twin sister."

"Oh," Alethea felt her heart sink.

Juana placed a hand on Alethea's shoulder. "Climb and stay hidden. I won't be far away, I just need to check some things out."

Nodding, Alethea began to climb the tree. At least being in the Night's clothing made that easier. It had been hard enough when she'd been in the short chiton of her youth.

Thinking of her youth brought back memories of times with Eramaus, and also the days without him. Alethea settled into a spot in the tree where she felt hidden from a quick glance up. If someone wanted to find her, it probably wouldn't be hard. All the more reason, she supposed, she would need to learn to defend herself. Though given these women, she'd not stand much of a chance. But would having learned to fight before made her any better in the eyes of Tara? Just how bad was Brisa if she had nearly started a war?

War.

The word hung in Alethea's mind as her memories raced. Lady Katica, Lord rest her soul, had said something about a war. Alethea gripped the tree as she tried to remember. The emperor had a second wife, Prince Lyrcus's mother, but his first wife was Prince Sarpedon's mother. And she had died in the Holy Land. One of the Night had killed her, and the Gran Mamara had told Alethea that the appropriate punishment had been dealt.

So, Alethea reasoned, given Juana's statement, it could have been Brisa who had killed the former Empress as revenge for her sister's death. She swallowed. And the woman had only been banished? Alethea was certain a mistake of that sort would have been punished with imprisonment, if not death, by the Light. But, she sighed, the Night didn't see things the way Light did. Alethea had not missed the excitement in her new friends' voices when they talked of the family they would be seeing at this Gran Fete. So perhaps, to them, banishment was a punishment worse than death. But if there were other people like Tara's mother, who still visited Brisa, how effective of a punishment was it?

Letting out a long breath, Alethea readjusted herself in the tree. It really wasn't worth the trouble trying to think of these things without the others to discuss them with.

"Lord of Light and Lady of Night," she spoke quietly, "guide my friends and help them find the right. Illumine and enlighten them."

A soft breeze rustled the leaves and Alethea felt calm. She could do this—be a child of the Night, blessed by the Light—and make all things right. And she dozed, feeling strangely at peace, until her world began to vibrate.

Tumbling forward, Alethea's hand shot out to grab hold of a branch to catch herself. Her heart pounded as the seconds wore on. There was no one about. No one was trying to kill her. Why did the ground shake? Why...

Alethea cautiously made her way around the tree to look southeast. The tremors had stopped, but the Holy Land's mountain smoked. How many times was that now? Three? Once for Lady Katica's Death, once when she'd been attacked in her tower, and now.

"Lord, please tell me they aren't making bad choices again."

There was a sad chuckle from around her. *Two choices have been made, one good, one poor. Their waywardness will soon be too great to ignore.*

"Aletia!"

Juana's voice brought Alethea's thoughts back from the Light. She looked down as the young woman looked up.

"I am fine," she told Juana as she began to clamber down.

Juana nodded. "There's a more hidden spot for us to rest in. We'll go to the Gran Fete tomorrow."

Alethea followed Juana as they carefully made their way to a den made by yellow flowering bushes. Juana set herself up by the 'door', while Alethea nestled near its multiple trunks.

"I do not like the way the ground shakes," Juana muttered. "It is your God, is it not?"

Alethea nodded. *But what about the Night, are they better than the Light, given what Brisa has done?* she wondered.

Their troubles are different and yet the same, the feminine wind whispered. *Tread carefully my child, for unrest is coming and my wrath will be harsher.*

Chapter 8

ജാള

In the morning, they followed the path Toli had taken the day before. The grassy land extended a ways up the mountain side, but it soon gave way to the jungle trees Alethea was more familiar with. The path wasn't hard to follow, though it had been worn by passersby rather than maintained with sand, shells, or rocks as the Light would have done.

"The first group traveling from Viamas to Damadiosa for the Gran Fete must cut a path," Juana explained when Alethea remarked upon it.

They continued in silence, listening to the forest noises. Soon those became eclipsed by roaring water. The sound cut into Alethea's mind, making thoughts hard. They stopped at the edge of a gully where a rope bridge began. A quick glance below to the roiling water made Alethea wish she was back on a boat.

Surviving a storm at sea seemed far easier than surviving a tumble into the torrent below. She swallowed. Three thick ropes made a V. Vines laced vertically between them with thinner ropes woven in horizontally. Alethea could only stare at it.

"Go on," Juana spoke loudly next to Alethea's ear. "It's repaired every year by the keepers of Damadiosa." She gently pushed Althea toward the ropes.

"I've never," Alethea began as she gripped tightly to the two higher ropes, her feet refusing to step on the third.

Juana pulled her away, shouting, "Watch."

Like a feline, the young woman walked with a deliberate pace down the lower rope, her hands out for balance over the top ropes. She easily pivoted and came back.

"Easy!" Juana grinned, gesturing for Alethea to go forward. "I'll wait till you cross before I go."

Taking a deep breath, Alethea reached forward once more, willing herself to place one foot on the lower rope. She moved a hand, the other clutching the rope tight. She brought her second foot onto the rope before the first. Bit by bit, Alethea made her way across. If she could conquer her fear of the sea, could survive nearly drowning twice, she could cross a river on a rope bridge. How was she to become like the Night if she couldn't? Clearly Juana was practiced at such a task. Alethea paused, closing her eyes for a moment as she reached the middle.

"Lady of Night," she spoke quietly, "give me strength to cross. Enlighten-me."

Peace filled her, coming from inside out. Alethea loosened her grip on the ropes and continued. Though she was still slow, she felt more confident. After all, this wasn't nearly as hard to do as running across the beam in the Tower had been. Sure, if she'd fallen off that and died, it would have only been a different death than the one she'd been running from.

The thought made her heart ache for her friends of the Light. At least she had made new friends and wasn't totally alone. And though she wasn't officially The Lord's Bride, she suspected she still had to keep her promise. Her eyes glanced up. If she was keeping her promise, then The Lord best keep his. First, she would learn the ways of the Night. And maybe she could figure out what *would* bring the Night and Light together. Maybe not all of them, that had to be impossible, but some, enough. And then, if Eramaus was still alive…

No, she swallowed her tears. The Lord promised he would live, so long as she did what he asked.

And with more gumption than she thought she had, Alethea picked up her pace, focusing on the solid ground at the other end of the bridge.

₲⇒∣

Juana crossed the bridge in a quarter of the time it had taken Alethea, and they continued forward in silence. Cresting a hill, the visage made Alethea pause for a moment. The land sloped down, dipping into a shallow gorge. Along their side of the riverbank, the even sided structures of the Night spread out in a haphazardly organized fashion. Similar, she thought, to what Viamas was like, but bigger, much bigger. The build-ings and walkways were on taller posts, water rushing around some of the furthest from them. Smoke rose between the clus-ters of huts, hinting at the promise of food. They were back in the plains now, tall thick grasses waving in the rain scented light breeze. Further up the hill, to the north of the village, pale yellow-green of the willows marked where the Healing Home was. But this wasn't a village, that was a Light term, and it was much bigger than Viamas. Did they also call this a tribal center, or was there a new word to learn?

"Damadiosa," Juana stated before Alethea could ask, "site of the Gran Fete held every twelve years in which all the clans and tribes gather?"

"All of them?" Alethea asked, eyes widening.

Juana chuckled. "Well, representatives of each tribe and

clan."

Ahead of them, a group of men carried filled baskets. Juana cleared her throat as they approached, and the men silently stepped to the side. Food, Alethea noted as she got a look at the contents. Toli had often foraged to bring back roots and berries, since they didn't have gardens or fields. None of the men looked directly at Juana or Alethea, though she felt their sideways glances.

"Have you seen Toli?" Juana asked one of the men in front.

The man did not look up when he answered. "No, not since he arrived yesterday."

Juana nodded and she and Alethea moved onward. Alethea felt their curious stares following her, and she tried her best to walk with the confidence Juana displayed. It didn't take long before they began ascending the nearest ladder-like stairs to the first platform of Damadiosa.

The sound of falling water caught Alethea's attention. Up-river, past a giant tree, the water fell down a tall cliff into the river flowing beside Damadiosa. She was glad this river didn't roar as the one they crossed had. Juana led her around hut clusters, working their way toward the tree. It was always, Alethea noted, an even number of huts encircling an even sided cooking hut.

That thought was quickly replaced as the sound of staves hitting each other caught her attention. She looked to her right as they turned left to see the practice platform. There was nothing on the other side of it, and she could feel the water rushing beneath it. A web of ropes and logs extended from the far side to the tall bank across the water and back. The women had only practiced in the afternoon in Viamas. The midday meal, so far as she could tell, hadn't been served, yet there were already women sparring on the platform below, and others making their way across the ropes.

Alethea caught up to Juana as she rounded one last group

of huts. The massive tree Alethea had seen before now rose directly before them. Its branches arched out, roots dangling from them, woven into what was clearly a hut. A hut with a massive trunk on the inside that she could see through the wide openings that let in breezes and light. Juana paused to glance at Alethea at the foot of the few steps up to the platform the living house sat on.

"Banyan tree," she whispered. "It's been growing since before the Great Divide. This is where the council meets, and where the Gran Mamara lives when in Damadiosa. Stay two steps back from me."

Nodding her consent, Alethea paused to make distance as Juana strode to the door. The young woman pounded her staff on the platform with a resounding thud that echoed. In its wake, even the waterfall seemed silent. There were people inside. They glanced to where Juana stood tall, but did not acknowledge her. Juana pounded her staff again, standing straighter than Alethea thought anyone could. She wished Toli was here to whisper explanations. Pounding the platform a third time, Juana finally got one of the women to rise and stride to the door.

"I bring the Gran Mamara's honored guest to greet her," Juana stated, still tall and proud.

"*Honored* guest?" The woman pursed her lips, raising her eyebrows.

Juana stepped up, planting her staff with another resounding thud. "Honored Guest, as tradition states, it will be done. I recommend you let us pass."

"But," the woman sneered, "what if I don't?"

"You will have breached tradition, Lara." Juana's voice was firm and strong, and Alethea was certain it was meant for those inside as well. "And in breaching tradition, all who wish to may challenge you." Juana's voice grew quiet, and Alethea barely caught her last words. "How many of us do you think you can win against before you fail? I know I won't be the first, and I doubt I'd be the last."

Lara smirked, her own words quiet. "You should listen to the people more, Juana. You might find things have changed." Her words grew louder, as if again speaking for those inside. "Let's not *break* tradition, but as you can see," she gestured sarcastically as she stepped aside, "the Gran Mamara isn't here."

"And where is she?" Juana asked, frustration leaking through.

"In the Healing Home." Lara's slow smile made a cold chill traverse Alethea's spine. "It seems she has the worst case of Viamas Penance the poporos have ever seen. Though perhaps it is a poison brought by the Burnt One?"

Alethea felt Lara's judgmental stare and swallowed.

ℹ

Droplets of rain fell timidly as they walked away. Alethea tried to imitate Juana's confident pivot and stride, but her insides tumbled with doubt. She'd never be accepted here. What was she thinking? Even when they had reached the ladder stairs that led to the Healing Home, Alethea could feel the heat of their hatred.

Lord, and Lady, she added, *I really hope that bringing these two peoples together won't be the death of me, because it really feels like it's trying to be.*

There was no answer from The Lord, or The Lady, and Juana stood silent, watching the poporos move about. She didn't move until a figure broke off, moving toward them. Alethea followed, concentrating on not falling off. Once she was down, she looked up and recognized the figure. Toli beckoned them silently toward a building. As they got closer, Alethea realized there were two Healing Homes. Passing between them, Alethea could hear coughing coming from inside. Toli stopped them before a grove of tall willow trees. Beds had been woven from their branches to hammock the elderly. Viamas hadn't had such a thing. In one, shared between trees, the Gran Mamara reclined. A man, a poporo, Alethea corrected, crouched beside her, mixing something in a pot over a stone brazier. His face reinforced the concern showing on Toli's. If the Gran Mamara was this sick, why was she out here among the elements?

The Gran Mamara turned from them as her body spasmed with a coughing fit. Juana waited until it finished before she struck her staff on the ground with a soft thud.

"Gran Mamara," Juana addressed the woman, "I have brought our honored guest, Aletia, as requested."

The Gran Mamara began to cough again, turning from them. The man hovering by stood, offering her a cloth. She wiped her mouth and shivered. Alethea wanted to help the woman, but she couldn't think of a way. At least not a way that didn't use her 'demon sorcery'.

"Thank you, Juana, please take your place." The Gran Mamara gestured to a spot next to her.

Juana did as she was asked, sitting cross-legged, her staff now laying across her lap as if she might at any moment spring forth and fight someone.

"Step up and nod your head," Toli whispered.

Alethea complied, and when the Gran Mamara reached out a hand, Alethea took it.

"Welcome, child, to Damadiosa. Given the situation, I must insist you stay with Toli's Grandmother, Amadora. Toli will lead you there before he returns to his duties."

Toli bowed. "As you wish, Gran Mamara."

The Gran Mamara fell into another coughing fit, and the man beside her gave her whatever he'd mixed up. She made a slight face but took it before looking back at them.

"Go. I will be well enough soon, and we may speak and

discuss much later."

Toli nodded, then turned and touched Alethea's arm.

"This way," he whispered.

As they left, Alethea felt the rain once more. A glance back showed that the ground was dry beneath the willows. She caught glimpses of the other poporos. At least not all of them sneered at her.

Chapter 9

ಐಂಬ

Toli wove them between the groupings of huts until Alethea was certain she was lost. By the time they stopped, her hair was dripping down her back. Glancing to the cooking hut, Alethea noticed that only four of the six spaces were in use. Just like there were four huts in this cluster, not six like in the others. Nor were there supports waiting for two more huts to be built.

Toli's rapping upon the door frame brought her attention to the hut before her. It stood wide open. "Grandmother," Toli wrapped again, "I request entrance for myself and our honored guest." His words were spoken clearly, though with slight hesitation.

"*Grandmother* isn't here." A woman stepped into the door-frame, blocking their way. She gave Toli the barest of glances before scrutinizing Alethea.

Alethea pulled herself up, trying for the confidence Juana had. The same that Lady Katica had tried to instill in her.

"Mother," Toli's voice was soft, "the Gran Mamara—"

"I know what the Gran Mamara said," the woman bit back

at him. "Doesn't mean I like it. And you shouldn't either. At least Tara has more sense in her,"

"Galena," another voice called from the opposite side as a staff pounded on the floor. "Behave yourself and let them in."

The woman clamped her mouth shut and moved away from the door. Alethea stepped inside, but the woman caught Toli and fiercely whispered something to him that Alethea couldn't quite catch. Galena moved outside with him. Glancing back, Alethea saw a look of pleading on his face, though not directed to her. When she glanced forward, she saw a soft face of understanding from the woman who'd just spoken. That woman turned to Alethea as Toli scurried off, his mother marching in another direction.

Like the Gran Mamara's hut in Viamas, there were partitions of blankets. Most were tied to the poles so that the whole house was filled with breezes and light from all the windows. She turned to the older woman, who now examined her. Despite her age, she was lithe and, Alethea was certain, could break her in two if she desired.

Swallowing, Alethea gave a hesitant smile. How was she supposed to greet her? She'd know what to do if they were Light, but Juana had only been formal here, so very unlike Viamas.

The woman snorted. "Have they taught you anything yet?"

"Well, um," Alethea fumbled for words to address the woman. "I had two broken legs, and, um."

The elder woman chuckled. "I heard that, though I see you have at least learned our language. I wasn't sure if I should believe it when the Gran Mamara said you spoke it well. Have you learned anything else?"

"No," Alethea shook her head. "I did ask how to be useful, but they said my skills are all wrong, and haven't taught me anything. Though, Tara said I should be trying to fight."

"And you haven't tried?"

"I, I only just stopped using crutches."

"Well, no time like the present to start."

Next thing Alethea knew, she and the woman had short staves in hand.

"Follow my lead."

Alethea swallowed and did as best she could to mimic the poses and movements the elder woman went through. Again and again, they repeated the stances and the movements. Sweat formed on Alethea's skin as, again and again, the elder woman corrected her posture and fluidity.

"She's bad." Galena spoke from the door as the elder woman took the staves back. "Even one of the men could best her."

The elder woman snorted. "You were that bad once. We all must start at the beginning."

Toli's mom took a swing at the elder woman. She dodged it and rounded on Galena, her short staff suddenly in the other woman's face. Toli's mom grimaced.

"I am still the Matriarch," the elder woman smirked. "Why don't you make sure the men are making enough food."

Her short staff stayed poised until Galena walked away again. The elder woman turned back to Alethea, holding out a hand. Alethea took it.

"I am Amadora. Do not mind my daughter, Galena. She is still bitter about her cousin's banishment, though it's been years. Come and rest with me, you have done well in your first training, but there is much more to learn."

⸙

Alethea trained using the shorter staff and with the children. The girls giggled at first, until the Matriarch berated them for insulting the Gran Mamara's honored guest. After all, it wasn't Aletia's fault her parents hadn't trained her properly.

And it wasn't just fighting Alethea learned, there were fluid movements of dance and the stories that went with them.

Stories that spoke of the Great Divide, when the Gods fought and broke the world in two, creating the Dark Barrier to separate the Night and Light. Nothing Alethea had learned with the Light dealt with why they were darker and stouter than the Night. The Night, however, told how The Lady had blessed the Night, making them pale like the stars and tall like the trees.

Five days passed before Galena was asked to test those who had been training at the hut. Alethea wasn't the only one aggressively knocked down. Amadora snorted.

"HAIT!" She pulled her daughter aside. "You think Tara got her aggression elsewhere, but I see the same in you; the same as your aunt saw in Brisa. Watch that hatred doesn't make you an outcast like her."

Galena snorted before looking to Alethea. "Don't suppose *you* did something to Tara to make her run away." She glared.

Taking a deep breath, Alethea won against the urge to shrink back. She raised her weary head to meet the woman's eyes. "I did nothing deliberate to chase her. All my actions have been to ensure our safety and nothing more. I am not here to cause division."

"Too late," Galena harrumphed as she stormed off to sit and wait for the coming meal.

"You cannot deny," Amadora spoke to her, "that her tale is the same as Toli's." But Galena had turned away and the family matriarch sighed. "Come," she gestured to Alethea, "sit with me."

Galena glared as Alethea moved to sit on the top tier. Matriarch Amadora frequently picked one of the younger girls to sit with her. It was usually one who had worked hard, or overcome a difficulty, and Alethea wondered if Galena had ever been honored this way. Surely the woman had worked hard as a child to learn the same things Alethea was learning. Or had she shunned all but the fighting? Still, the honor felt odd, and Alethea felt the other women's stares as they entered for the meal.

Amadora pounded her staff on the floor once they were seated. "Aletia is the honored guest of the Gran Mamara. She is here to learn our way as her predecessors did before her. When the Gran Fete is over, she will take our ways to help the Light improve theirs."

Whispers ran around the room. Alethea sighed, muttering softly in Light, "~If they don't kill me first.~"

Amadora patted her knee as Alethea was offered the meat bowl first. She smiled at the man, who was easily Amadora's age, quietly thanking him as she always did. He returned her smile, offering the meat bowl to Amadora. Back home, Ada Mos served everyone, because Light women cooked and served while the men worked the fields or manned the boats. But no one tended any fields here. They preferred to hunt and gather what they needed. And clearly Night women hunted and Night men gathered.

So much about the Night was opposite the Light, her brain couldn't process it all. The stories and training helped some, but Alethea had seen nothing that explained how they worshiped The Lady of the Night other than the silence that settled over Damadiosa at dusk. She'd hoped being with the children might let her ask questions, but even they did not question the Matriarch.

Heaving a sigh, Aleatha finished her food and rejoined the girls for archery. This time they were going to make a trip into the woods to try and hunt.

Alethea was strapping on her quiver when a knock came at the door.

"Juana," Galena spoke, a cross look on her face as she moved to the openeing. "You should know Tara isn't here, and hasn't been for days."

"I know," Juana replied flatly. "I am not here for Tara."

"I suppose you haven't found her, either."

"I have not looked for her since the day she left."

"She *was* in your charge."

"And *you* know as well as I, Galena, that she was not entirely happy being in my group. Being capable of hunting and defending herself, she is allowed to leave, should she desire. Without warning."

The two women stared at each other until the Matriarch's staff pounded the floor. Galena's scowl deepened, but Juana looked past her.

"Matriarch Amadora," Juana spoke, "I am here to escort Aletia to the Gran Mamara to speak to her at length."

Galena continued to block the door until Juana's and Amadora's staves thudded. Stepping aside, Galena gestured sarcastically for Alethea to pass. Alethea began to undo the quiver and hand over her bow, but the Matriarch shook her head slightly. Juana's staff resounded against another as Alethea passed Galena.

"She is the honored guest of the Gran Mamara, Galena, so I suggest you treat her as tradition dictates." Juana took her staff away. "Breach it, and see who will challenge you. I guarantee there will be more than you can best." Juana smiled. "Have a lovely afternoon." She nodded to the Matriarch who nodded back with a tiny smirk.

Alethea followed Juana, quiver still on her back and bow in hand, puzzling over what the girl had said. Juana's confidence when addressing those older than her was flabbergasting.

"Do," Alethea asked softly, continuing once Juana had glanced at her, "do people really challenge each other over breaching tradition?"

Juana stopped and turned to face Alethea. "Do the Light not do the same?"

"No, not really. Disagreements are brought to the leaders who listen to all sides of the story before passing judgment." Alethea thought for a moment. "At least that's what I was taught. I've never seen it. My father had to go before a leader to do that a few times."

"The Light are weird."

Juana grimaced, continuing to lead Alethea to the Healing Homes. Being after lunch, they passed many women going in the other direction. They were likely the afternoon group heading to the training grounds. Many glanced their way, looking more at Juana than Alethea. She wondered if having the bow and quiver made her blend in a little better. Or made her a little more acceptable, for there was an occasional burning glance and hiss at her. Someone whispered *burnt demon*, but they hurried away with one beat of Juana's staff. Silently sighing, Alethea wondered if she'd ever find more than a handful of people who accepted her.

Fighting the tears that sprung to her eyes, she straightened up, emulating Juana's posture as much as she could. A soft breeze caressed her skin, *Your hardships will be rewarded, child.* But was there even a reward that could make up for the heartache that constantly plagued her? She wanted to see her friends again. She wanted to be with Eramaus. But what if they no longer liked her? Or worse, a sob nearly broke from her chest, were dead because of her.

Engrossed in her spiraling thoughts, Alethea nearly stepped off the edge at the steep stairs. Taking a deep breath, she concentrated on going down frontwards like Juana. She followed Juana between the Healing Homes, only to be bared by a poporo. Alethea was certain he wasn't the same one as before.

Juana planted her staff on the ground, taking a step forward. The man took a hesitant step back, worrying his hands.

"The Gran Mamara is not accepting visitors." His eyes glanced from Juana to Alethea nervously.

"Tomayo, the Gran Mamara told me herself that she wished to speak with *our* honored guest," Juana stated.

The man looked behind him at the woman next to one of the woven beds. Juana pushed past the man as the figure turned.

"You should not be here, Lara."

"The Gran Mamara is terribly ill, Juana, I doubt she wants—"

"Jealous that she chose me for her champion instead of you?"

"Fine," Lara brushed past Juana, "have it your way. But you know who they blame for her illness." Her scathing gaze buried into Alethea's soul.

The man glanced at both Juana and Alethea. At Juana's nod, he left.

For a moment, It was quiet. Then coughing from the hanging bed drawing their attention.

"Come," Juana motioned Alethea forward as she backed away. "I will stand watch."

Alethea nodded. It seemed odd that the Gran Mamara was out in the open like this. The Light kept their sickest in darkness. Though she'd learned that some light was better than none, so much light and air couldn't be good either.

"Toli," the Gran Mamara croaked, and Toli rose from some hiding place by the tree trunk. "Prop me up," she paused as she coughed, "then bring my tea."

"Yes, Gran Mamara."

He nodded as he pulled cushions from around her and helped her sit up. There she perched as if on a throne of willow and pillows. But instead of looking regal, she looked pale. Alethea wondered if she would even be able to use the staff that Toli lay across her lap.

"Come, sit child," the woman rasped.

Alethea sat on the ground before her, suddenly reminded of the frailness of Lady Katica. She reached out to touch the old woman's knee.

"I can heal you," she whispered, "I—"

The Gran Mamara waived off her words.

"Toli has told me of what you did for yourself, and I am aware of the miracles The Lady of Light can do. But the poporos are doing their mending, and that is enough."

She turned as another coughing fit overtook her.

"Are you sure?" Alethea looked up at her. "I just do not wish to lose you as I lost Lady Katica, before I learn what I need to know." She found herself wrestling with rising despair.

The Gran Mamara reached out a hand and patted Alethea's head. "Do not worry, I am not as sick as the poporos seem to think I am. I plan on living a nice long life. After all, neither of my successors have had grandchildren."

"Grandchildren?" Alethea blinked in surprise.

"Yes," a cough wracked the Gran Mamara's body. "Unlike the Light, we believe a woman must know how to fight and have been a mother and a grandmother before she leads. This way she understands the things that face her charges."

Alethea nodded. "I have witnessed birth and death."

"But as Lady of Light you will not give birth, nor lie with another. I have argued with Lady Katica about your ways. It is pointless to continue the argument."

Another coughing fit left the Gran Mamara breathless.

"Surely you could let Aletia mend your cough." Toli approached with a tea pot and cup in hand. He poured the pungent liquid into the cup and handed it over. "It's weakening you, and the rumors—"

The Gran Mamara waved him quiet as she took the cup and drank deeply. She grimaced.

"I could pray for a temporary reprieve," Alethea stated. "Just to lessen the cough. And I can pray to The Lady. She said she'll answer my prayers the way The Lord does."

The Gran Mamara shook her head and smiled gently as she reached out to Alethea. "Do you understand why I cannot accept your healing? Especially not here?"

Alethea frowned. "It would break my trying to fit in." Alethea cocked her head as she thought. "If I cannot go back to the Light, I must become one of the Night. As Night, I can only mend. But I can't mend, either, because that's the job of poporos as it is the job of the mediki of the Light."

"That is certainly part of it." The woman nodded, taking another draught of her tea. "But I am also their leader, in thought, word, and deed. So, I must uphold our traditions."

"I am so far behind knowing what I need to know as a Night of my age. I can't fight, or hunt, but there must be some help I can offer? I feel I'm not good at anything."

The Gran Mamara smiled at her. "Oh child, I think you will find that is very much not true."

That dusk, even though the Gran Mamara had told her not to, Alethea prayed silently. *Lady of Night, please see fit to give the leader of your people the strength to overcome this illness that her people might see all is well. Enlighten-her.*

She looked up as something streaked across the sky, and felt a hand take hers.

"The Lady blessed us," a quiet child's voice spoke.

Alethea glanced down to see one of the little girls of Toli's family. The girl turned her eyes from the sky to Alethea and hesitantly smiled.

❧◑◐❧

A strangled sob woke Alethea that night. The girl who'd taken her hand that evening bit her knuckle to keep from crying out. In the shadows outside, Alethea could see a woman knocking one of the men about. As he crumpled into a ball, the child's sobs nearly came undone. Without thinking, Alethea reached for her, and the young girl rolled over to bury her face in Alethea's shoulder.

The woman gave the man one last kick and walked away. Alethea swallowed. She walked as Alethea had seen her father walk when he had too much to drink. The woman didn't come back into the hut, simply meandering off someplace else. The girl whimpered.

Alethea stroked her hair. "Shhh, the woman's gone."

"But my father," the girl whispered. "Has he gotten up? I, I'm not allowed to help him. I'm too big, they won't let me be with him anymore. But maybe, maybe you can?" She glanced outside, then into Alethea's face. "You're the Gran Mamara's honored guest. They can't scold you."

The man lay still, though Alethea could see his chest move. Not a single person in the hut stirred to help him. Nor did anyone appear from any of the huts nearby. Alethea doubted she'd get out of a scolding if she was caught. Looking down at the pleading eyes of the child, she nodded.

"We'll both help," she whispered.

Why did they separate the men from the women so much, Alethea wondered as the two of them crept outside. Toli had seemed more integrated with Juana and Tara than the men did in this house. Was that why she was staying here? To see the backwardness of it? But just because it contradicted nearly everything she experienced with Light, didn't mean this way was wrong. Maybe there was right and wrong on both sides. Beating someone for no reason was just as wrong no matter who was beaten or who was doing the beating.

The two of them cautiously crouched beside the groaning man.

"Papa?" The little girl spoke softly, touching the man's

hand.

"Maria?" His head moved, his eye catching sight of her. "Go back to bed, you should not be here."

"The Gran Mamara's honored guest is with me. She can do anything."

"Gran Mamara's honored guest? Child, it, that, doesn't..." He shifted as Alethea gently touched his left side. "Lady?"

Alethea blinked.

"Lady, please, do not let it be my time, not with my child watching."

"She's not," but the girl gasped slightly as she gazed at Alethea. "Lady of Night, I, I'm sorry, I didn't, I shouldn't."

The girl's sobs were barely contained, and Alethea remembered losing her own mother at a similar tender age. She brought her other hand to lay hovering over the man's body as warmth and tenderness filled her. Her skin glowed like a night sky filled with stars.

"No child should be kept from a parent they love," she whispered, memories of her own loss at the child's age rising within her. "What you ask in love should be granted. There should be no need to fear asking. Nor should you fear losing your father to unwarranted violence." She paused, turning her hand up to the sky to catch the starlight. "Lady of Night, heal this man and make it right, Enlighten-him."

Tipping her hands, Alethea let her glow traverse onto him, and when it was gone, she sank, hanging her head. Weariness of mind washed over her, different from the weariness of body from prayers to The Lord, and she found herself weeping. She barely noticed the man rising as his child helped her back into her bed to sleep until dawn.

Chapter 10

A constant, though thin, plume of smoke rose from the Holy Land over the course of days as Eramaus helped clear out debris from the quaking earth. At least this wasn't as back breaking, or as heart breaking, as clearing the tower. Captain Boreas had insisted that all his mercenaries help. Those who hadn't, found themselves wanting a new job.

In fact, one day he came back from his labors to see Emelye standing in the shadows wearing a kolobus. She constantly yanked on the hem of it, looking from the Captain, who was conversing with two mercenaries Eramaus didn't know, until she spotted Eramaus. She strode over to him.

"Hey, Eramaus," she tried to deepen her voice, only to squeak slightly.

Eramaus blinked. "You best play mute," he told her. "And stop fussing with your kolobus."

"It's so short," she complained, keeping her voice quiet. "I still don't understand why—"

"You're the one who told Captain Boreas you'd be able to fight as well as a man if someone would train you."

"I didn't think he'd take me up on that."

"Ah, Eramaus," Captain Boreas cut into their conversation, "come bring yer cousin Emil over to meet tha group."

Eramaus gave Em one more quick admonishing look before they went to meet the gathered group. A group in which he only recognized Basil and Giles.

"Now, Emil's a bit green, so he'll stay back with Eramaus since he's gotten *official* training." The Captain smiled at his crew.

Emelye did her best to be Emil. And tried to stick to keeping quiet, though Eramaus could see her bursting to talk. Basil and Giles, however, judging by their winks and nudges knew what was up. At least they didn't mind sparring with her, despite her being a beginner. It really was no surprise that he and 'Emil' were put behind the second to last wagon, with Giles and Basil on the last. And, of course, it was drizzling.

"You would not guess what our favorite vapid little viper is up to," Emelye burst out after they had gone a ways from the city.

"Gaining high mediki so she can be the *new* Lady of Light?" Eramaus sighed. Lowri would be a revolting Lady, creating havoc instead of peace.

"Oh, no, at least the high psara council has more sense than that. But you are right about her becoming High Mediki. And yes, that did happen right around the time the world shook."

"So why is she—"

"Swines in a blanket, you are so dense sometimes," Emelye huffed. "She *originally* went to become Prince Sarpedon's bride, because Daphne was to be Lady of Light, but then Alethea was anointed. Now they seem to be going back to the original plan. I have no idea how she finagled that."

Eramaus raised his eyebrows at her. Lowri was not beyond using her body to get her way. Emelye pursed her lips.

"Right. Not going to think about that." His cousin shuddered.

"So, what you are saying is that High Mediki Daphne is going to be Lady of Light and Lowri," he grimaced, "is going to be empress? That bodes *oh* so well."

"Well at least I heard the Basilica is so damaged it will take years to fix—"

"And there's some sort of fissure," Eramaus interrupted with a smirk, "keeping her from getting married in the Holy Land."

"Maybe the Night will kill her like they did Sarpedon's mother."

"That's one way to start a war." Eramaus's mood tumbled back. He was already ready to murder people for taking Thea away, and if the same people took his mother, or Emelye…

"What are we supposed to do?" Emelye moaned, interrupting his thoughts. "How do we fight to keep Lowri out of power, Eramaus? She probably has people out looking for us, and—"

"Do you think we still matter to her?" Eramaus raised his eyebrows, glancing at Em.

"You're right," Emelye sighed. "We *were* her key to crushing Alethea, but I doubt she sees us as useful anymore." Emelye dramatically put the back of her hand to her forehead. "Cast off again are we."

Eramaus rolled his eyes and paused for a step. "Do you really think Thea is still alive?"

Emelye dropped her pose and placed her hands on her hips. "Yes! You really *are* the densest!"

ഔരെ

Alethea didn't see Maria's father again. But Maria followed Alethea like a shadow, sticking close to her as much as she was allowed. Amadora gently scolded her to go home when she followed them to the practice grounds a few days later.

"But I want to see Aletia assessed."

"You'll see her compete soon enough, mija," Amadora said kindly as she shooed the child away. "But you have your own practice to do."

"Compete?" Alethea swallowed as her voice squeaked.

"Hopefully. Presuming you are good enough, of course." Amadora smiled as they continued on. "We'll need to be careful who we pit you against, but all the girls of your age compete." She sighed. "You have learned much in such a short time, but we will see. Or you could break a leg and have the poporos declare you unfit to fight." She winked.

For a moment, Alethea wished she hadn't healed herself so well. But it was probably for the best. She had to try to be accepted.

They sat two rows up from the sparring platform, watching as the girls took their turn on the practice ground. Women who looked close to Alethea's age walked among them, judging them. The rest sat on the benches chattering with the elders and each other. If Alethea closed her eyes she could almost have been among the Light.

Not quite, she thought—there was an accent. So many words seemed the same, though they sounded different. If only the Night wrote the way the Light did, Alethea could figure it out. Certainly, given how different the two were, some words of the Light, like guard, road, or kolobus had no translation. But they also had some things which Alethea couldn't translate into Light, like clan and tribe, or the watchers who could commune with the animals and trees.

"Aletia!"

The sound of her name brought her back to the platform. Amadora gestured for her to go down. Her gut sank as she took up her position. She faced a girl about her size, but perhaps a little older.

"Really? The half staff? You should grow up and use a real staff."

"It's what I know," Alethea stated, trying her best not to cringe.

Most of Toli's family, especially those who trained with her, liked her. She'd become comfortable with them. She just wished she could spend more time with Toli. He was the only one who really shared her curiosity about the other side of things. But it was taboo for a woman to spend time with a man training to be a poporo.

Movement in her peripheral snapped Alethea back into focus. She dodged, but didn't manage a parry. Her thoughts flew to the barest whisper as she tried to hold her own against the young woman.

"You fight like a boy," someone in the stands called out.

"Get on the offensive!" another voice cried.

Soon, the two of them had a cheering section. Rather, Alethea had one cheering section and one degrading section. Not that she could hear the words. Her ears rung with the crashing of staff on staff. Time was an endless whirl of wood.

Until a solid hit spun her, followed by another to the back of her knees, bringing her down. Time stopped as she teetered on the edge of the platform, staring into the water. Her opponent's staff tapped the back of her head.

Alethea held up her arms in an x above her head. She was defeated. Someone took her staff from her. Breathing deeply, Alethea slowly rose. As she turned, her foot slipped. A hand shot out and caught her before she toppled into the river below.

"Hey, no dying during practice."

Alethea looked up into the face of a massive woman. Her grin looked familiar.

"That was practice?" The words squeaked through her lips

without Alethea meaning them too.

"Ahh, mana, you are funny!" The woman nearly doubled with laughter as she pounded Alethea on the back. "I see you might not have the skill of a warrior, but you have the heart." Her laughter died down, though her grin was still present. "I think we met in Viamas, in the Healers' hut. You broke the wall trying to walk."

"Coleta?" Alethea placed the name Toli had called her.

"Aye." Alethea couldn't help but smile back. "Good to officially meet you, Aletia." She grasped Alethea's hand and shook it. "Now, I best go knock some sense into your opponent there before the grand mistress calls me out for being lazy." Coleta winked and gently gave Alethea a shove toward the stands before she moved to where the girl Alethea had lost to stood waiting.

Alethea walked back up to where Amadora sat. The woman looked to her and nodded.

Twice more, Alethea went out that day, and again once more the next morning. Each time returning to the bench in defeat where Amadora would give 'helpful' comments about the current fighter's techniques. Alethea was glad that second day when they left just after lunch to sharpen spear heads and arrows. And even then, all the information she'd received tried to drown her like the ocean once had.

౩)(౪

The next day dawned with sunshine and an excitement Alethea couldn't place. She'd never seen so many men of Night on the walkways. They hurried hither and thither, gathering things, exchanging things, only to disappear then reappear to do it again. By mid-afternoon, the flow of men had diminished, but the smell of food in Damadiosa increased. It was fruity and smokey, and her mouth began to water.

Their morning training had only consisted of going over forms. And even the oldest of the girls Alethea was with couldn't seem to concentrate on them. The sound of drums made them all stop. Half the children ran to put their staffs away without a call from Amadora. The Matriarch smiled and nodded to the rest that they could do the same. No sooner was her weapon away, than Maria grabbed her hand with a squeal.

"It's Feast Time!"

Alethea was half dragged, half pushed by Maria toward the practice grounds. Long tables were set up on the sparring platform, tended by the men who were serving people. Other men hurried back and forth. There was so much food, and so many people, Alethea froze looking at it all, uncertain of where she should be.

Maria ran off with other children her age. In a cabana on the upstream side, Alethea saw Juana with the Gran Mamara. Should she go there? She was supposed to be the Gran Mamara's guest, so sitting with her would make sense.

She wove her way through the groups of people. Some stood to eat, while others sat on the tired benches around the practice grounds. She was almost to the cabana when she heard her name.

"Aletia!" Coleta's hand waved at her from a few rows below.

Alethea hesitantly returned the wave.

"Come get your food with us, Aletia!" The big woman beckoned her to where they were, now another row lower.

Alethea glanced at the Gran Mamara, who nodded.

Coleta was still standing and waving. "Come on, before the good stuff is gone!"

Bewildered by the invitation, Alethea weaved her way through the crowd to Coleta. She noticed that men were sitting among the women. Young children sat with peers, or their parents. It was such a mix of people, so unlike the clearly tiered structure in the hut where age and gender were on distinct levels.

"Mana!" Coleta draped an arm around Alethea's shoulder as she caught up to her. "Meet mi otra manas."

Alethea looked at the other faces in the group. There were a few boys there, including Toli. She smiled, and he smiled back. Coleta kept Alethea at her side as they got food and made their way to a top tier of benches. As the group ate, their talk revolved around who was interested in who, and the new babies from the clans of the Night.

"Am I right in thinking the Gran Mamara brought everyone out?" one of the girls asked, looking at Toli.

He said nothing but gave a little nod.

"Then why did she bring an honored guest?" The young woman looked at Alethea.

Toli swallowed as all eyes turned to Alethea. She stopped eating, glancing about the group. They leaned forward, eager to hear her speak. How much could she tell these people? Toli she trusted. But what about Coleta? Or the others whose names she didn't know? Did the Night have the same sort of people who schemed and desired power.

Oh yes, the wind whispered to her. *It is in the nature of people. though we have tried to guide it out of them, they still exist.* The wind sighed.

"She does speak our language, doesn't she?" A boy asked, looking at Toli.

"I do, I just..." Alethea swallowed.

Coleta put an arm around Alethea to give her a light squeeze.

"We should *walk*." The woman put an odd emphasis on the last word.

Everyone nodded, and silence enveloped them as they finished eating and dispersed.

"Come," Coleta took hold of Alethea's hand, "I'll show you

some of the good places."

Glancing to the cabana where the Gran Mamara had been, she saw only an empty box. Someone else touched her, and she looked to see Toli. He smiled and nodded at her before disappearing. Next thing Alethea knew, Coleta took her arm in hers and they began to stroll.

They weren't the only ones wandering to the outskirts of Damadiosa. Hide shelters had sprung up almost overnight, and people were laughing and talking, or doing things that made Alethea blush and look away. Coleta chuckled when she did that. At first there seemed to be no plan to their walk. Coleta chatted, pointing out this and that, waving to people. They wove far from Damadiosa, almost to the trees, before Coleta wound back to a place between the Healing Homes and the Gran Mamara's tree hut.

"Come." Coleta pointed up into the branches of a tall tree.

With an ease of practice Alethea envied, Coleta vaulted into the branches.

"You'll need to help her," Juana's voice came from the branches above.

Coleta's face appeared, upside down and grinning. Alethea was beginning to wonder if the woman ever frowned. Next thing she knew, the girl who'd asked the questions boosted her up to Coleta who easily brought her the rest of the way up. A wide platform was suspended between the branches. Toli was already there, along with Juana. The other woman quickly joined them. Silence descended on the small group as Toli brought forth sweets from his bag and they settled into a circle.

"You wished to discuss something, Salina?" Juana asked the other woman.

"Why did the Gran Mamara bring everyone from Viamas? This is unprecedented, and clearly not sanctioned by the Council." Salina glanced to Alethea. "Nor was she expected. Is she even *the* honored guest?"

"It was not safe to leave anyone there," Juana stated.

"So, we all saw The Lady's Peak steam, did the stream run dry as well? And has it not happened here too?"

Juana opened her mouth to speak and then closed it. She looked to Alethea, and they all looked to her. Juana glanced back at Salina. "You asked if she was *the* honored guest. I think it is wise for her to tell you why she is, but is not."

"She has the words to do so?" Salina's gaze did not falter from Alethea's face.

Alethea felt her cheeks heat. "I do, I think."

Toli patted her knee. Coleta squeezed her hand. For a moment, Alethea closed her eyes, gathering her thoughts. "By honored guest, you mean I must be the ~Lady of Light~?"

Juana nodded.

"Which I am and am not." Alethea paused to gather her thoughts again. "~The Lord of Light~ did pick me, as did the former ~Lady of Light~, but," she tried to find the right words, "the people in charge did not want me."

"Why not?" asked the young man who had wondered if she could speak Night.

"Well," Alethea chuckled nervously, "I look too much like you." She gestured to them. Salina scoffed and Coleta chuckled, but Alethea shrugged and continued. "The leaders of the Light, they gave honor and power to, uncaring people."

"Wait, the ~Lady of Light~ isn't the leader?" Coleta looked at her, astonished.

Alethea shook her head. "She's more a, um," Alethea tried to figure out the right word, "she gives advice. But there was no way I could be as wise as Lady Katica. I'm so young, so, so," again her Night words failed her, "so new to the world outside my hut." Alethea swallowed, trying to not cry, to remain strong like a Night woman.

"They tried to kill her too," Juana spoke up. "That is part

of why she is here, or perhaps the Gran Mamara would have waited till the next Gran Fete."

Salina snorted. "By next Gran Fete, Lara would have her place. She's scheming for it now. Rumor is she's working with Brisa." The young woman looked to Toli. "Any word on your twin?"

He shook his head.

"Has this not been taken to the council?" Coleta asked. "Lara is not a grandmother. She must wait till the first grandchild is over five years old. And if she's talking with the banished –"

"It's been mentioned." Salina nodded.

"Let me guess," Toli quietly spoke, "and they will not deal with it until the Gran Fete is over."

"Do they ever deal with things during the Fete?" Coleta asked, popping a sweet into her mouth. "We'll bring it to the Gran Mamara. You can get us in to see her, right Juana?"

"Coleta, the Gran Mamara has been ill. She is recovering and needs to rest as much as possible before the final fights. Why do you think I came to speak with you?"

"Because you have a soft spot for Toli?" Coleta grinned.

"As my potential major poporo." She glared at Coleta.

"I wish she would let me heal her." Alethea sighed, her words not meant to be aloud, or in Night.

"When did you offer?" Juana asked.

"The day you brought me to see her."

"Did anyone hear you offer?"

"Just me," Toli stated. "The Gran Mamara wouldn't let her, even though she knows Aletia could cure her."

"So, the Light can," Salina paused for a second, "make people whole?"

"No, um, just me," Alethea fidgeted with her skirt hem, "or, well, maybe it's a gift given to all Ladies of Light? The Lady of Night said she'd probably let Toli do the same but, I—"

"Born of the Night, made Lady of Light!" Coleta exclaimed, her hand slapping the platform they sat on. "Are we to follow you into the sun?"

Everyone shifted to face Coleta and the young woman looked excitedly around at them. For a moment there was utter silence, before Juana laughed a little.

"Yes," Juana spoke, "I knew it in my heart the first time I saw her." She nodded at Alethea. "The Gran Mamara believes it too." Juana shook her head. "I have tried to speak to Lara about it, but she, she won't listen."

There was a long pause, broken at last by Salina. "I think she's been talking with Brisa. We all know she didn't agree with the Gran Mamara when she cast that woman out of the Tribes."

"I fear that's where Tara is too," Toli whispered. "My mother has never fully stopped seeing her."

"Who'd Brisa kill again?" Coleta asked.

"~The Empress~," Alethea stated, which only got looks of confusion. "The next most powerful woman among the Light. Not that women have much power." She offered a weak smile.

"The equivalent to murdering the Gran Poporo." Juana clarified.

Salina shook her head. "Most outcasts are peaceful people. They mind their own business and give no trouble. But Brisa's been raiding villages these past few years, and she's only getting bolder. Some of the clans have indicated that people have gone missing after Brisa was heard to be in the area."

"I don't like this," Juana sighed. "But I'm not at all sure what we can do."

"Follow her into the sun?" Toli asked, gesturing at Alethea.

"I don't think it's going to be that easy," Alethea stated.

"But you are born of the Night, right?" Coleta asked. "And were Lady of Light."

"When a child of the Night," Juana spoke, "becomes Lady

of Light, old wounds she'll heal and try to make right. But when the lakes steam and the waters run dry, the end of the beginning is nigh. When you follow the chosen into the sun, know that our peoples will now be one."

"And at least one mountain has steamed," Salina added.

"And the stream in Viamas ran dry," Coleta stated.

"I saw the shapeless statue that lay behind the waterfall," Toli whispered.

"You're not supposed to look on that," Salina scolded. "No one should see the image of The Lady."

"I saw it too," Alethea spoke up as Toli hung his head. Their judging stares turned to her. "I, well, I thought I was dead." She gave a weak smile. "Look, the Light, we, they have a similar prophecy." She looked at the group as the wind ruffled their hair. They had light inside. Alethea could see it glow. Not light, she realized, but love. *All Love* The Lord had told her. "The Lady of Night and Lord of Light were never at odds. It's been the people all along. We *are* one people, only we've all forgotten it."

"But the story of the Great Divide," Coleta looked concerned.

"I know," Alethea half sobbed. "And I don't know how I'm to get past that hatred. Not to mention, I don't even know what I'm leading you all out of or into. And," she took a deep breath, trying to soothe her frustration, "I just, need to understand the Night first."

"Bonfire!" Coleta beamed.

Juana nearly choked on the sweet she'd just bitten. Once she swallowed, she reached out to pat Coleta's knee.

"Curb the enthusiasm," Juana stated. "Lara isn't the only one who doesn't like that Aletia is here." Salina nodded assent. "But since you've clearly 'adopted her'," Juana broke a half smile as Coleta threw an arm around Alethea, "you best keep her safe."

"You got it, mana."

‟‣

Coleta led Alethea back to Damadiosa, where they paid their respects to Matriarch Amadora and Coleta let her know she was taking Alethea to the Bonfire. Amadora gave a similar caution as Juana did, though phased much softer. Back outside, Coleta wove them through the huts to another ladder stair. That was the third, if not fourth, Alethea had been on. They hadn't gone far when they were joined by some of the others from the feast. The group kept getting bigger and louder the further they went.

Remaining silent, Alethea did her best not to panic. Neither Juana nor Amadora seemed to think this was a bad idea. But Alethea had no idea what would happen at the bonfire with so many people present. She didn't even know what women of Light did to amuse themselves, let alone what the Night might do. She'd spent her time in prayer, mending things, or watching others do things. Or following Eramaus. But there was no Eramaus, just Coleta.

As the party moved, Alethea fell further behind. Coleta had been handed a drink, her arm long since gone from Alethea's shoulder. Looking back, Alethea could barely make out Damadiosa between the trees. Dusk was falling and the moon was slowly rising. She looked up in that moment of silence as the stars began to appear. Part of her quaked a little inside.

You shouldn't be out at night, you should be safe in your bed, lest The Lady of Night spirit you away and turn you into a slave.

But other than the men serving, Alethea hadn't seen a single slave.

She stopped as a bright bonfire came into view. She knew she was here to learn more about the Night, but what was here?

She was certain the gourds were filled with a fermented drink. She'd gotten away with refusing it at the feast and wondered if she could get out of it here. Why did she refuse it? What was she afraid of if she drank it? It wasn't like she'd be the only one drinking from one. Surely no one would poison her with it. Alethea swallowed.

"Aletia?"

Alethea jumped at Salina's voice.

"Where's Coleta?" the young woman asked.

"Um," Alethea looked about, "there?" She waved vaguely in the bonfire's direction.

As if on cue, Coleta spun out of the group that was starting to dance around the fire.

"Aletia!" She bounded to them. "Oh good, thank you, Salina."

"You are supposed to be protecting her," Salina scolded gently.

"Yes, yes," Coleta nodded. "Come, Aletia, have fun. Tomorrow, we rest, and then The Games."

"Yes, The Games," Salina echoed with a chuckle as she rolled her eyes.

Wrapping an arm around Alethea, Coleta pulled her into the firelight.

"The Gran Mamara's Honored Guest!" Coleta announced.

If anyone heard her, they didn't care, or pretended not to. There was a shadowy figure across the way whose eyes bored into Alethea, as if she was some kind of plague. Alethea sighed, finding a drinking gourd in her hand. She looked at it for a moment. What was she afraid of?

"Drink, it is good!" Coleta encouraged.

She'd already survived at least three attempts to kill her. So, she drank. It was not wine. It had that same tang as wine, but it was sweeter, like fruit. Coleta took it from her, taking a swig before passing it on to the next person.

Next thing she knew, Coleta was dragging her into the dancing. Many of them cheerfully offered her instructions on how to move her feet. Some of it she'd learned already with the young girls, but there were more complicated moves on top of the basics.

"Where did you grow up?" Alethea recognized the voice of her first opponent at practice. "Among the Burnt Ones?" The young woman and her friends laughed.

She reminded Alethea of Lowri. Be strong, she told herself as she swallowed. Do not let them take your authority, Lady Katica's advice echoed in her head. But what authority did she have here?

"So, what if she did." Juana jumped from a tree branch into the group, standing between them and Alethea. "What would that matter when she has been invited by the Gran Mamara?"

"My great-grandmother barely remembers the last time a Gran Mamara invited an honored guest. How do you know she's not just saying that to make you believe it?"

Juana slapped her forehead. "Just because it hasn't happened in a long time, doesn't mean she's trying to fool us." Juana turned to Alethea. "Tell me, Aletia, why hasn't there been an honored guest in a long time?"

Alethea blinked at Juana. What did the girl want her to say? "Well, the last, um, honored guest, was very old and I, I was only recently—"

"Lies!" the girl interrupted, moving forward.

Alethea's eyes drifted up and she sighed. *Lady? These are your people, a little help would be nice, please enlighten me.* She refocused to see the insulting girl another step closer.

"She will never believe us, Juana." Alethea shook her head, as reverberating words poured through her. "Her mind has been made, and in this bed she will lay. For even should The Lady of Night appear, she and her friends would not hear." Alethea looked sadly at the confused woman. "I pray no ill befalls you." And she stepped away, not quite turning her back, but dismissing the woman just the same.

Coleta looked at Juana, then Salina, then Alethea, before breaking into a grin. Once more Coleta's arm was about Alethea's shoulders and another gourd in her hand. But as the night progressed the group slowly split into two. Just like, she thought, the way the Light and Night had. But those thoughts tapered off as she drank and danced, her fear of asking questions dissipating. She wasn't certain what question it was she asked, but whatever it was got them calling for Juana.

Juana appeared, jumping down as she had before, nimble on her feet. Had she drunk anything from the gourds? Maybe she was trying to be more vigilant. She was training to be a leader, because the Gran Mamara was a leader, right? Alethea's thoughts tumbled in her head as she swayed.

"The Flood to Divide, Flood to Divide," the other girls stated. "Tell us of the beginning!"

Juana frowned as the chant continued.

"Please?" Alethea's voice broke through the chant.

Juana glanced at her, cocking her head. At last, she nodded into the breathless silence. A cheer rose as they all gathered like children for story time. A gourd was offered to Juana and she took a swig.

Who in the sea keeps providing them? Alethea wondered as another went around the group.

"The Flood to Divide?" Juana asked them.

"Yes!" they all shouted. Even some who had been sitting on the other side, talking amongst themselves, ignoring Alethea, responded.

"All right." Juana smiled as her gaze passed over the group. Kind of like how Lady Katica would.

"In the beginning,..." Juana took a stance by the fire, her story told in gestures and words.

Alethea listened in fascination as Juana unfolded a tale. It began similar to Light's—a world created by water, the islands rising from the sea. But for the People of Night, they were stars floating on the water. For Light they were birthed by the kiss of the sun on the ocean. In both people's tales, the Sun and Moon walked among them. Here it was all Night, there it was all Light. Both spoke of the argument that broke out between the Sun and Moon. Alethea stopped comparing, for here the two diverged.

Juana's flow mesmerized her as she listened to how the Moon wished to return to the sky and the Sun wished to stay upon the earth. But the Moon argued that the Sun's rays were hurting the land around it and the land needed him to rise. And he complained that she too did naught but laze away her days with the people who were not worthy of them. But they were her children. And so she rose, making the land rise with her. The Sun tried to burn her land.

But some of the children sided with the Sun. They liked his rays, didn't understand the need for the world to be as it was. And the waters rose. But the Moon used the sun's heat against him, turning the shores black. And for forty-two days they battled, their children hiding from the destruction and pain. And with one final thrust, the Moon launched herself into the sky, sending the Sun to its opposite side creating the cycle of night and day. And before the Moon, The Lady of Night, left the Holy Land, she told them fear not, for death may be a part of life, but from death life will always rise. And so, the Dark Barrier did not remain black and burnt by the Sun for long, and showed the people of the Night that her words were true and there would always be life from death. So even when the forest burns, it is but renewing itself, and making a space for newer and better life.

Alethea sighed as Juana ended. "I like that version better."

"What version do you know?" Coleta asked, making Alethea regret her words nearly immediately.

As Alethea stuttered, Juana walked over. "Another time perhaps, Coleta. It is late, and I do need to bring her back."

"Bah, it's not late at all. There is still time before the sun rises."

Alethea looked, and, sure enough, the sky had grown lighter and the bonfire was slowly dying.

"I do not think Alethea is ready to take part in the morning salutations. It is, after all, her first Gran Fete."

There was a sigh that ran around the group, but no one protested again as Juana led Alethea away.

Chapter 11

ഇൗരു

Coleta was correct that the day after the bonfire was a rest day. No one practiced, just nibbled on whatever food was around. Alethea found herself collected by Coleta sometime in the afternoon to just wander about. It struck Alethea how like Knight Anchises and his squires the group was. Coleta reminded her of a younger Eramaus, and Alethea's heart ached for him. She wondered, then, if Juana was Knight Anchises, though she was on the younger side of the group.

Still, with all of them, Alethea felt protected. They were cautiously curious, occasionally asking her quiet questions about the Light. In return, they answered her questions without judgment. She learned a lot more this way than she had with Amadora. They explained the tribes and how the tribes were split into clans, and the clans into families. And when they said family, they didn't mean just parents and children, they meant three or four generations living together in one hut. The Matriarch ruled until another woman of the family challenged the Matriarch and fought her for it.

Tomorrow was the start of The Games. There would be

matches of skill, and potential changes in matriarchs. They spoke a lot about the competition of non-mothers, since they were all in that group.

"Juana and Coleta will clearly be the final fight," Salina said.

"Don't throw the fight this time, eh Coleta?" one of the others joked, jabbing her in the ribs.

"What?" Coleta's eyebrows raised. "Juana is better than her age group. She should fight with the mothers."

"She can't," Salina reminded, "until she has a child."

"She has to be a mother to fight in the next group up?" Alethea asked quietly.

Salina nodded to the muttered ayes, and yeses of the girls around her.

"What if, what if you don't want to be a mother?" The question came out though she didn't mean it to.

But Salina caught it and laughed. "Then you'll be like Coleta, regulated to training the young."

"Or trumping their butts." Coleta grinned.

Alethea nodded, thoughts rolling about her mind. Women of Light were also expected to bear a child, though a man of the Light didn't need to have a child to gain his family's status. Odd, that, even for the Night, a woman had to give birth to at least one child to be a matriarch. And, beyond that, your child had to have a child to be on the Tribal council, or to become the Gran Mamara. Most matriarchs, it sounded like, were grandmothers. And they generally had a daughter old enough and strong enough to support their rule, and fight for them in cases where they could not. And those daughters usually became the next matriarch of the family via a formal fight. So, then, girl children were wanted by the Night, while the Light wanted boy children.

"Is Jauna's family here?" Alethea quietly asked Salina.

"No. She lost her family in the Great Sickness." Salina

spoke sadly, "When they brought the orphans to Damadiosa, the Gran Mamara picked her to be her heir. Zorida had disappeared, and Brisa, well…" Salina trailed off. "Anyway, the council made the Gran Mamara take Lara to be next in line, but she's appointed Juana to be her champion."

಄಄ೞ

The day began with pouring rain, though that didn't dampen spirits. Alethea noticed families gathering in clans after the loosened structure of the last few days. Awnings had sprung up all about them, providing some respite from the rain. Alethea was given a seat next to Amadora, and all the women sat in the same row or behind them, with all the men of the family behind them. Toli was, of course, with the poporos at the side of the platform.

Alethea recognized a few of the girls from those she'd been training with in the hut. They went across the wet stage in waves, showing off their short staff routines. She wished Galena was seated further away. Toli's mother made incessant remarks about the children's performance, clearly trying to get a rise from Amadora. Amadora ignored Galena as she cheered the children.

The next day was much the same, only the girls were young women around Alethea's age. Though there were drastic height differences between the youngest and oldest, all of them used the long staff. In addition, these girls also scrambled across the web of ropes and logs. Alethea spotted her two sparring partners among the group. Watching the whole group made it clear that neither of them were good. In fact, some of the younger girls were better. Alethea wasn't sure if that knowledge made her feel worse or better about her own skills.

"Tara should have been out there," Galena grumbled as everyone began to filter back to their huts that evening.

"Tara has not been home," Amadora countered.

Galena stalked off, not staying in the hut for dinner that night. Thankfully, like the night before, it was a light repast. The men had ensured the women had ample food and drink while they were watching. Alethea was glad none of it had been the strong fermented drink she'd had the night of the bonfire.

Loud cheers rang out on day three as women came to take the stage. It was so much louder, Alethea instinctively turned and saw the men standing, joining in the excitement. Turning back to the stage, Alethea tried to determine if there was a meaning to the women's arrangement. Perhaps skill, she thought, as she caught sight of Juana and Coleta standing on either end of the front row. Salina stood in the row behind them. The row bowed to the steady beat of a drum before moving off to a location behind the poporos. The next row stepped up and left to the opposite side. Each row alternated until the last row bowed. Instead of walking off they all marched into positions.

"HAIT," A voice rang loud and clear from the Gran Mamara's cabana.

Alethea quickly glanced to see Lara up there before her attention was brought back to the platform as the first long staffs clashed. This was no organized display of skill. These girls were clearly sparring with the intent to win. It became clear with the first knockout, as to why the poporos were there. No sooner had the girl gone down than two poporos rushed out to bring her back to where they were stationed.

"HAIT," rang out once again after all the fights ended.

The women quickly raced to take their places on the ropes as the next group of women took up the platform.

"HAIT," rung out once more signaling the chaos to begin.

At the end of that round, the girls in the ropes went to the side opposite the poporos and took up bows. With three things going on all at once, Alethea didn't know where to look until Salina came out, her group followed by Juana and Coleta's. She wanted to cheer for them, but families only cheered for their kin. Still, her eyes flicked back and forth between all three.

Salina failed to win her sparring match. The girl's arms shot over her head, conceding the fight just as all the ones around her finished. Coleta and Juana won both of their sparring matches. On the ropes, Coleta's big frame hampered her, at least compared to Juana and Salina. In archery, Alethea was certain that Salina was the best, though it was hard to judge when Juana and Coleta weren't there at the same time as her. Juana definitely beat out her group. She heaved a sigh of relief as the event ended, and her stomach grumbled loudly.

Amadora laughed. "Come, back to the hut, the men will have food for us."

As they were joined by that day's combatants in the hut, a keening sound rose from a hut nearby, startling Alethea. She looked about, but there was only a short pause before conversation resumed. A small hand found its way into hers and she looked down to see Maria. The child looked up at her, eyes glossy with sadness.

"Grandmamma told me sometimes people die, and that The Lady will take care of them. Will you take care of them, Lady?"

Alethea moved to be on the child's level. "I am not The Lady, but," she paused for a moment, feeling the wind caress them, "She says She will."

For a moment, the two of them stood there, until someone called something out and Maria let go of Alethea's hand and scurried off.

୫ා୨

When they came back to the platform that afternoon, the group that presented itself was much smaller. Alethea had no idea how they figured out who, other than the ones that lost the initial fight, was eliminated from the competition. Juana, Coleta, and Salina were still in the mix of women though. This time they stuck to the long staff and did not go on the ropes or do any archery. After each round, losers were removed, and the women regrouped.

Salina was knocked out after five rounds, but Juana and Coleta stayed strong until the final round where they faced each other. Alethea found herself on the edge of her seat as she watched her friends battle. Coleta's herculean frame dwarfed Juana's lithe form. But what Juana lacked in power, she made up for in speed and agility. Juana would duck, pivot, and hit as Coleta methodically tried to strike her. The sound of their clashing long staffs echoed against the cliff of the river-bank. People cheered for every good hit, not seeming to care who won.

Maybe it was because Galena wasn't cheering that Alethea noticed pockets of people conversing quietly, not watching the fight below. Glancing at one group, she had to glance again. But the figure she thought was Tara had vanished. And Toli was clearly still with the poporos. A wild cheer brought Alethea's attention back to the platform. Coleta lay prone, Juana standing over her, long staff touching Coleta's throat.

"Bah," Galena spit out as she rose. "Coleta let her win."

Amadora turned to berate her daughter, but Galena was already gone.

She didn't return that night, and Alethea didn't see the woman until she took her place on the platform the next day. There were once more groups like the day before, in lines. Galena was in one of the lines near the back. Amodora sat silent next to Alethea all that morning as they watched. She cheered for none of her family, though Alethea was certain there were two others from their hut on the platform. The day played out much as the last one did. At least it started out that way, but these women used spears. Elimination was by drawing blood from your opponent, or knocking them unconscious, keeping the poporos busy.

The men served food and drink mid-day, but no one returned to their huts as they had before. Instead, the women were organized on the platform while everyone watched. As the fights progressed, the injuries became more intense. Alethea found herself clutching at her skirt, twisting it into knots, her hands clenched tight. She cried out as a woman lost her balance at the platform edge, plummeting to the water below.

The crowd gasped, and Alethea heard Amadora whisper, "The Lady has chosen."

But The Games went on until Lara stood as the final victor. Only then did Alethea look up to see Juana standing in the Gran Mamara's cabana. She'd not recognized her voice shouting out HAIT. As they moved back to the huts with the setting sun, Alethea sent a silent prayer out to The Lady of Night to bring health and mending to the Gran Mamara. And she sent out a silent prayer for those who keened tonight, for the sound came from more than one hut.

Chapter 12

◈

Why there was no village here, Eramaus didn't know. Gorgomilos wasn't much further from the Pass, and no Night had bothered them. Still, there were trees somewhat evenly spaced to make a good camp circle for trading caravans. He watched Emelye spar with Basil. Basil and Giles liked teaching 'Emil' swordplay, and Eramaus was trying hard to tell if there was an underlying reason for it. They might not have called Em out for being a guy in disguise, but sometimes they said things that led Eramaus to believe they fully knew.

"That's enough," Eramaus called out, standing so that he could intervene if necessary. "We've got a long day tomorrow to get over the Pass and into Gorgomilos."

"I'm not sure I can sleep," Emelye/Emil said, her voice not staying deep, again. "I'm kind of excited."

Basil and Giles exchanged puzzled looks even as Eramaus spoke. "It's nothing special."

"But maybe we'll see some of the Night." She turned to him. "Did you ever see any on your jaunts to the Holy Land."

"They weren't jaunts, Em," Eramaus spoke through gritted

teeth as they all came closer to him. "I was there to protect Thea Lady, not that it did much good. Well…" He trailed off remembering how his quick thinking had potentially saved her life the day they tried to assassinate her.

"All right, but did you see any of the Dark Ones in the Holy Land?" Giles asked.

"Yes, and as you two know I've fought the *Night*," he emphasized the term, "in the Pass."

"The *Night* eh," Basil caught on.

He glared at him *and* Giles until the two left for their own rolls. He was about to do the same when he caught sight of Emelye staring at the black rocks.

She sighed dreamily. "Women warriors."

Eramaus rolled his eyes and then nudged her as Captain Boreas came over to them.

"Eramaus, Emil, good, you are still up," he said once he was abreast of them. "Now, Eramaus, seeing as you have been to the Holy Land with Alethea, have you met the Night out of combat?"

Why did people have to harp on this? Eramaus's glare at the question was met with a kindly face. He sighed. "Yes." He'd promised Thea not to say anything about that time he met the boy Toli and the Gran Mamara, but…

Emelye punched his shoulder. "You lucky goose!"

"Look, Em," he rounded on his cousin, "I just…" He paused as he remembered there had been another encounter. Eramaus turned back to the Captain. "Remember the one the others wanted to kill, but I couldn't?"

"Aye," Boreas nodded.

"Well, I saw her at the top of the Pilgrim's pass, and she, well, thanked me."

"She spoke Light?" the Captain asked.

"It was broken," Eramaus nodded, "like she didn't know much, or had only learned those words."

Boreas nodded. "Now, I've placed yah back here for reasons. One, as yah might have figured, is Basil and Giles are Bleedin' Hearts. But two, 'cause you'll need to help 'em when we stop fer lunch. We'll stop right at the top a'for heading down. It's ta rest the beasts n'such, but also ta leave goods ta pay for passage. Now, the Night should attack to cover the drop, but tha Captain of the caravan that went through the pass a few days ago said they didn't attack him. I don't care if they do o' don't, but you two will help Basil and Giles an' ensure tha 'precariously' perched bag gets out into the road. Once it's dropped, the fighten' will stop."

"Have they ever not attacked when they should have before?" Emelye piped up.

The Captain shook his head. "And I can't tell if it be good or bad, but I ain't going to go back on an arrangement that's been in place since a'fore I were born."

By the time they stopped for lunch the next day, even Eramaus was glad for the short respite. Emelye kept looking to the steep banks that rose to either side of them as they ate. But there wasn't even a rustle of the jungle leaves before Captain Boreas called down the line to move out.

"They didn't attack," Em sighed.

"It's better that way," Eramaus grunted as he helped Basil drop the bundle.

Knowing Thea was half Light, half Night, and having seen them help her when she'd been attacked by the Light, Eramaus wasn't sure he could fight them anymore. He might as well let the Night kill him like the Light had killed Thea.

"Don't worry, Emil," Giles's voice broke through his morose thoughts, "we can spar later."

Eramaus glanced at Giles, trying to read his expression. But neither Giles nor Basil said another word until they arrived late that night in Gorgomilos. The Captain gave them all a small advance and most of the men went into the city.

Eramaus and Emelye opted to stay with the wagons. The city reminded him of how his father ignored him and his brothers tortured him. He'd rather stay where he'd seemed to matter.

Of course, Giles and Basil also stayed behind. After all, Giles had promised to spar with 'Emil' so 'he' didn't feel disappointed by not fighting the Night. Not to be left out, Basil took the first turn.

"Shame Emil has to go at it like he does," Giles remarked as they watched Basil spar with Emelye.

Eramaus glanced to the man. "Sh—"he caught himself, "Em's going at it like we taught him."

The man gave him a half grin. "Not that way, the other way. But I suppose it be safer fer Em to go this way. *He's* got some spitfire."

Eramaus narrowed his gaze at the man. "Em's my cousin, and don't you dare," he growled, then grinned slyly. "'Sides, Em's got my taste in women."

Giles blinked and stared hard at Eramaus's face. Eramaus remained smiling.

"Right, then," he nodded. "Point taken."

With a shake of his head, Giles moved off to switch places with Basil. Giles's shift in attitude was clear as he and 'Emil' sparred, and Eramaus heard Basil's interested 'huh'.

"Oh my gooses, I'm cooked," Em laughed as her sword came flying out of her hand. "I swear I could sleep through a whole day now."

Giles laughed as he fetched the sword, then beckoned to Basil, saying they'd bring back some food and drink.

"I swear he worked me harder than ever."

And she'd called him the dense one. Still, Eramaus said nothing.

⁖☃

There was a solemness to the next day of The Games, though Alethea wasn't sure she would call anything in which people died, Games. The gray clouds above provided shade, but the mist made Alethea shiver. Yet, all the families gathered except for their oldest and youngest members. Alethea wished it would rain and be done with it.

Lara was back in the Gran Mamara's cabana. She called forth all the matriarchs of the families. Amadora and a good two dozen other women stepped forward. Some had younger women by their sides. Once all the women were on the platform, Lara called forth those who wished to challenge their matriarchs.

There was a collective gasp from Toli's family as Galena stood up and walked down to the platform to join the dozen others. Alethea found Maria leaning against her, shivering, and Alethea brought an arm around the child, suddenly finding two more children taking comfort from her.

Each challenger was called to present a child. The children came scrambling over. Galena's voice was heard over the crowd commanding Toli to come forth.

"He can't be her child, he's training to be a poporo," one of the women near Alethea whispered.

"That would be true if he'd already given up his manhood, but you know she hasn't let him do that yet," another responded. "Probably never will."

"Lady, please let Gran-mamma Ama win," Maria whispered, eyes closed, clutching tightly to Alethea.

Toli dragged his feet, slowly making his way to Galena. He wasn't there long, and the moment he was dismissed, he scrambled away to the stands. Alethea caught his eyes as he passed. Tears leaked from them as he joined the men in the back. Maria's father put an arm around the boy and said something softly.

Maria's tightening grip made Alethea look back in time to see Amadora and Galena face each other in the middle of the platform. Three other pairs shared it with them, another four pairs stood at the ready on the start of the ropes course, and the final four pairs stood at the archery range, bows in hand.

"HAIT!" Lara's voice rang out, and wood clashed against wood.

Galena danced around Amadora like a child baiting a boar. But boars were mean and could take out a child. Alethea swallowed as Galena took a heavy stab at Amadora with her spear. Knocking the spear away, Amadora said something that could not be heard over the roar of the crowd, but Galena kept dancing, trying to stab her matriarch. Alethea was certain if one of her attacks hit, Amadora would be as good as dead.

Holding the children as much for her comfort as theirs, Alethea winced as Galena finally drew blood. But instead of that being the first of many, it became her first and last hit. Amadora morphed into a blur of action, her spear used as a staff, until Galena lost hers to the waters below as she teetered on the edge of the platform. With a resounding crack, Amadora brought Galena to her knees. Another well placed hit knocked the woman to the floor.

The family around her sighed with relief, the poporos scurrying forward to move Galena's unconscious form. Amadora looked to the judges, who nodded back to her in an unspoken agreement, before she moved back to take her place, greeted with solemn congratulations from her family.

"I made sure not to kill her," Amadora spoke softly for both Maria and Alethea to hear. "Though she won't be able to walk for a few days."

Alethea didn't want to watch any more, but the pairs switched up who was where. There was another woman who was knocked into the waters. Amadora sighed and Alethea glanced to see the older woman had tears in her eyes. She blinked them away and patted Alethea's shoulder, but said nothing. Returning her attention to the platform, she watched as the matriarchs of the last two groups raised their arms in defeat to their challengers, smiles on their faces.

"That is how it should be," Amadora spoke solemnly.

That evening was sober, broken by keening. They were midway through their evening meal when Toli knocked and was given permission to enter.

Walking up to his grandmother, he bowed his head before looking up. "Your challenger is in the Healing Home, under willow bark."

"As she should be." Amadora nodded, reaching forward to touch Toli's cheek. He winced slightly and Alethea noticed the welt on it. "You may stay with us, Toli," her voice radiated warmth as she sat back and watched him.

Toli once more bowed his head. "Thank you, my matriarch, but my duty is with the poporos."

"Very well," Amadora nodded. "I understand. Go with The Lady's Night."

"May her stars sing you to sleep," Toli responded before leaving.

Chapter 13

Alethea wasn't sure she wanted to sit through another day of The Games, but there seemed no way out of it as they gathered once more. Juana sat in the Gran Mamara's cabana and she called forth the major matriarchs. Ten women descended to the platform, three of whom had younger women by their sides. Once more, challengers were called forth. Six women descended, two of whom had just won matriarch status the day before. Alethea glanced at Amadora. The woman's lips were pursed, though she said nothing. Scanning the faces about her, Alethea noticed a few others with pursed lips. Another day of unexpected events, and Alethea's heart sank.

Each challenger was called to prove their grandmother status, and they in turn called forth a daughter, and in one case a son, who came with a child of their own. Some of the children were of Maria's age, but there were two who could not have been more than two.

"Tradition breach!" a voice called out from the crowd.

As others began to echo the sentiment, Juana called out for the challengers to take their place on the platform. And it wasn't long before Juana's voice called "HAIT" to begin the fight.

Alethea couldn't bear to watch it. The challengers pummeled the older women, who fought as if their life was dependent on it. There were no peaceful surrenders. And of the challenged major matriarchs, only the one who had a younger woman fight for her stayed in her position. All the way home that evening, Alethea felt the tension, hearing whispers about her.

"This is bad."

"They broke tradition."

"It's the Burnt One's fault."

"At least Lara doesn't have a grandchild yet," Amadora spoke quietly to her family as they ate. "Or Lady enlighten-us, there will be changes faster than a torrential downpour." She spared a glance to Alethea but said no more.

⋐⋑

Eramaus and 'Emil' were helping to unload goods outside Gorgomilos when a messenger rode by. It wasn't an odd occurrence, except that his pony bore trappings of deep purple with a white seven-pointed star. To make it worse, seven pennants of black were pinned to the reins. Eramaus wasn't the only one that inhaled sharply.

"I don't like this," Em stated, deepening her voice as much as she could.

She wasn't good at it, nor was she good at remaining quiet. Eramaus often wondered how many of the men had figured out her ruse.

"Nor do I," Giles muttered. "Royal deaths never bode well."

Many of the others nodded in agreement before going back to work. Eramaus sighed as he noticed his cousin slipped away.

"He does that ya know," Basil stated as he hefted his bag. "Usually comes back with good tidbits of information. Bit like Darian."

"Darian?" Eramaus hefted a bag into a man's cart once Captain Boreas nodded he could.

"Good lad that one." Giles nodded. "Could get secrets from bone, he could, if yah gave him time."

Both men gave Eramaus a thump on the back and moved to speak with the Captain. Eramaus stayed by his post, unloading and loading items when commanded. Kicking himself for not following Emelye to keep her safe, he hoped she knew what she was doing.

The Captain kept him busy until the evening meal, which was right about when Emelye returned. Trailed by Basil and Giles, she looked thoroughly disgusted. Basil held a rag to his nose.

"I don't know how that viper manages to enjoy what she does." Emelye flopped down next to Eramaus. "Men are utterly disgusting pigs. No, wait, that would be an insult to the pigs. They are much cleaner than everyone gives them credit for."

"Men can be too," Eramaus defended.

"Aye," Basil and Giles piped up.

Emelye just rolled her eyes at all three of them. "And has a one of you even *taken* a bath since we left Paramythia?"

They exchanged glances, none of them speaking a word. Seriously though, what was a few weeks of stench when everyone else stunk too?

"Well, you should." She looked to Eramaus. "What if we happened upon Alethea and she saw how unkept and stinky you are?"

Basil and Giles slid away, leaving him and his cousin alone. Eramaus sighed.

"So why were you using *her* methods? And on whom?"

Emelye turned beat red. "Not *her* methods exactly. Just,

you know, a little flirting, and a little extra alcohol. You know I can't stand being pawed at. I punched Basil cause he got in the way of my punching— Ugh," she shuddered. "Anyway, I got information."

"Information? What are *we* going to do with information, Em? You've already pointed out that we can't stop Lowri marrying Sarpedon any more than we could've stopped Poulos from attacking the tower."

Emelye sighed. "No, I suppose not. But I get the sense that not even Lady Katica knew how big and deep the Bleeding Hearts are. Maybe they *can* do something. Basil and Giles will tell Captain Boreas, and if they need us I'm sure—"

"So," Eramaus interrupted, "am I remaining in the dark, or are you going to share this information with me?"

"Well," Emelye huffed, "if you really want to know... Not that there's much to say. I mean we all guessed it when the messenger passed by." She sighed. "The emperor is dead. Apparently, he got sick the day we left the capital. I caught the hint that some feel it might have been foul play," Emelye coughed Lowri's name into her fist. "But anyway, all the princes are being summoned to swear fealty to the new Emperor and attend his wedding on the day of the Feast of the Sea."

Eramaus heaved a sigh. "She lost her patience. Think Daphne still has some influence on the Prince? Anchises thought she did."

"Ah, Anchises."

The two spun to face Captain Boreas, with Giles and Basil next to him.

"What about Anchises?" Eramaus asked, cautiously looking between the three of them.

"I know ye trust me, lad." The Captain placed a hand on his shoulder. "And I swear ye can trust these two lads as you do me. A messenger will catch up with Anchises before we do,

so I need ye and Em here to go with Basil and Giles to speak
ta him. He's tha closest thing to a leader the Bleeding Hearts
has now. And he needs ta know, from those who were there,
of the Tower's falling. I get the sense that news is being kept ta
rumors." He reached out to place his other hand on Emelye's
shoulder. "Can I trust ye both?"

Eramaus and Emelye nodded.

"Good. Ye leave tomorrow, but I need ye back in Valaora
by the twenty-seventh." The Captain dropped his hands from
their shoulders. "And Eramaus, ye be sure to leave time to say
hello to ye mother, it'll be on yer way back any how."

ℰⅭ

It was incongruous that the sun came out bright and
warm after so many days of overcast. The morning began at a
leisurely pace, though there were mutterings and soft talking
at breakfast. Yet anytime Alethea neared a group, they became
silent, giving her a wary stare. Between the overheard comments last night and their actions today, Alethea was certain
they'd decided she was to blame for all the upheaval.

I'm not, am I, Lady of Night? She thought as they settled on
their seats at the platform.

Not the cause, but a catalyst, the feminine wind whispered.
My people must choose their path as The Lord's people did.

They aren't choosing wisely, are they? Alethea asked with a
sinking heart.

There was no reply, but the crowd shifted, and Alethea
turned to see the Gran Mamara emerge from her cabana.
She strode to the platform, flanked by Juana and Lara. Even
though Alethea was nearly halfway around the platform, she
could tell the Gran Mamara struggled. She walked proud,
like Lady Katica channeling The Lord's strength, but her long
staff echoed on the platform, while Juana's and Lara's did not.

When she spoke, it was inaudible. Lara and Juana leaned in to hear, before Juana stepped forward to address the crowd.

"Has our new council been chosen?"

The women who had either not fought yesterday or who had won their fights stood and moved forward.

The Gran Mamara spoke again and once more Juana spread the word to the crowd.

"Then it is settled—"

"I think not," Lara interrupted as the crowd gasped. "Elrene, come show them my granddaughter!"

A woman rose, thin and pale. She cradled a bundle to her chest. Alethea could hear the faint cries of the infant. Juana immediately turned to the Gran Mamara who beckoned forth the council. There was a heated discussion in the circle, though none of the words could be heard. There were a lot of whispers about Lara, some good, some bad. Toli's family was split by the idea of letting Lara fight the Gran Mamara.

Alethea let out a breath as the circle of women broke. Relief washed over her until she saw Juana's face. There was a long pause as the whole audience leaned forward.

"It has been decided," Juana stated flatly. "The challenge stands."

Lara began to move onto the platform, pausing and looking back, her impatience clear.

"Are you certain you wish to do this?" Juana asked.

"Oh, I am certain. I think we *all* are certain."

Watch them, Alethea heard Lady Katica's voice in her head. Glancing to the council she could tell there was a divide. Those who didn't move were a minority compared to those who nodded, validating Lara's statement. A split, and a choice, just like the Light. Alethea bit her lip.

"So be it," Juana stated as the Gran Mamara gave a definitive nod. "As Gran Mamara Mari's champion and granddaughter, I will fight in her stead."

"Then the challenge is accepted."

There was no mistaking the scheming grin on Lara's face as she strutted into the middle of the platform. Juana spoke quietly with the Gran Mamara for a moment. Then she strode out and turned to face her opponent. Size wise, Lara was a more even match to Juana than Coleta had been, but how their skills compared, Alethea didn't know. And that mattered. Even if she hadn't heard Amadora's comment last night, she would have felt the concern in the air.

"This does not bode well," The Matriarch muttered softly. She turned to Alethea, leaning in. "If Lara wins, you run to Coleta and her group. They will keep you safe."

Alethea swallowed as her eyes flicked to the Gran Mamara. Toli brought her a chair, but stayed standing at her side. The Gran Mamara's brows were furrowed as she held her staff the same way Lady Katica used to, ready to hit anyone who displeased her.

"HAIT!" a councilwoman's voice rang.

Alethea turned her attention back to the platform. Juana and Lara circled each other, an occasional crack of wood against wood. Every other match Alethea had watched had been quick, attacks almost too fast to see. But these two were taking their time. Alethea wished she'd paid more attention to both Lara and Juana's winning fights from The Games. Not that she would know what a good move was like to save her life, but maybe, maybe she'd have a chance to understand what was happening. Furrowing her brows she studied the two faces. They were exchanging words too soft for anyone to hear.

"Get on with it!" someone cried.

"Fight already!" called another voice.

Juana frowned and Lara attacked. Juana blocked and returned with a strike of her own. Back and forth the blows went, now fast and furious. Occasionally, Alethea caught the base of a move she'd learned, only to have it spun into something more complex, more deadly if the other didn't counter. They took up the whole platform, pushing each other to the edges with leaps and rolls. Alethea felt dizzy watching them.

CRACK!

The crowd stood with a gasp. Lara's long staff was now two jagged-tipped short staffs.

"We should get her out now," Salina's voice whispered near Alethea.

"Bad staff made by a bad leader," Coleta whispered as Amadora said, "Wait."

Lara changed tactics. Two staves were hard to block at once. Alethea bit her knuckle as Juana's moves became more desperate. Was Lara trying to kill her? At least a half-staff didn't have the reach of the long-staff.

"She's pushing her to the edge," Coleta whispered, her arm now on Alethea's.

Juana swung her staff low, as Lara's toes touched the edge.

"She should have gone for the midriff," Salina cursed.

Lara jumped the staff, pivoting around Juana. Before Juana could react, Lara raked her across her back, drawing blood. The crowd gasped as Juana turned, the ragged edge of Lara's staff now pointed at her throat.

Juana froze, her eyes glancing to the Gran Mamara. The whole crowd pivoted to where their leader sat. Tara stood behind Toli, restraining him. But it was the woman who stood, with one hand resting heavily on the Gran Mamara's shoulder, that made Alethea go pale.

"Get her out NOW," Amadora hissed as she pushed Alethea behind her.

"Brisa," Salina hissed as she and Coleta pulled Alethea away.

"Lara is your new Gran Mamara," the woman's voice rang out, bitter and cold, "and I am her champion."

"Outcast!" someone cried out.

Her cries were taken up by others who surged forward. Salina and Coleta, kept down, weaving between the people. But the cries of outcast soon became cries of pain. Alethea chanced a glance back. Arrows rained from across the river's gorge. Her eye's met Juana's and the young woman smiled.

Go her lips said as she stepped, plummeting to the water below.

Go, the wind whipped about her.

Coleta threw punches. Salina went for knees.

"BRING ME THE GUEST!" Brisa roared as someone grabbed Alethea.

Stomping down hard, Alethea winced as bone cracked. She was let go, and she scrambled after Coleta and Salina.

The ground began to tremble as they wove between huts.

"Down!" Salina ordered as a walkway and hut intersected.

Coleta hopped down with ease, her arms stretching up. Salina handed Alethea down before leaping to the ground with cat-like grace. Others jumped down after them. There were shouts and curses and the clashing of wood.

Another violent tremor tripped her. She looked up, a spear inches from her face. Coleta fought someone as Salina helped her up.

There was a log before her, washed over by the waterfall.

"Go across! We'll follow."

Alethea chanced one look. Everything was chaos. Above them, a dark plume drifted across the sky. She ran, trusting The Lord and Lady to keep her alive.

Chapter 14

It was Giles's suggestion for Emil to go back to being Emelye. Eramaus wasn't happy with the idea, but he didn't expect Emelye's only protest to be that she couldn't train anymore. Basil had the brilliant idea that they would be traveling as Emelye's honor guard. Eramaus, of course, was her closest male relative, while Giles was the cousin of her future husband.

"Trust me," Giles whispered to Emelye, "my cousin has no desire to marry. But my uncle puts on a show of not being able to find the right spouse."

Basil would be the hired sword, an extra precaution against the jungle road. Unfortunately, they had to walk as the coin Boreas provided wasn't enough to get a cart. They'd been told that Anchises's route always took him down the northern road through Frasta and Smyria. If the messenger had told him about the Emperor's death, he'd likely be recalled as were the seven princes. Which meant he would have taken the road from Smyria to Gorgomilos, which meant he'd not pass through Valaora where Captain Boreas was going. Staying with Giles's uncle, who lived in Smyria, would be their best way to cross paths with Knight Anchises.

So, for two days, they trudged the road, swaths of jungle on either side. There was a way station halfway though. It was like a small walled town with a dozen or so buildings. There were more travelers staying there than Eramaus had suspected there would be. News traveled fast. Everyone was chatting about seeing the new Emperor's coronation, and maybe visiting the Holy Land. He and Emleye exchanged glances, and she gave a half-hearted smile and shrug. But neither said anything about blocked paths or fissures blocking their path to the Holy Land.

They arrived in Smyria close to dusk, hurrying the last hundred feet of cleared rainforest to make it before the city gate closed. Even though there were archers on the walls, it was still better to be inside before the night beasts came out hunting.

Eramaus glanced to Em as the gate shut behind them. She looked back and heaved a sigh of relief. They both remembered fending off an attack in Itea before being let in. They'd all been newly initiated, him a squire, Emelye and Thea mediki. They'd pulled some crazy prayers that night, and Eramaus didn't dare try now. After all, he was an ex-squire, and The Lord probably wouldn't listen anyway, not without Thea there.

Thea.

Emelye thought she was alive, had escaped. Eramaus barely allowed himself to hope she was.

"GILES!" A loud boisterous voice snapped Eramaus's attention back to the streets.

A heavy-set man, decked with bangles and jingles, and more decoration than could ever be considered tasteful, jogged up to him. How he jogged, and yelled, given the look of his physique, was beyond Eramaus's comprehension. The man started to hug Giles, quickly transitioning to grab his shoulders instead.

"Coming right off the caravan, I sense." The man's nose wrinkled. "And I suppose the bath wasn't available at the way station. Tsk Tsk."

"Sadly it wasn't," Emelye confirmed before Giles could answer, "or I surely would have made all three of them bathe after me."

She scowled at them as if it had been their fault there had been no bath available. Giles's uncle turned to Emelye and gave her the biggest smile.

"And this must be the delightful person you wrote of. Well, come come come." He bowed slightly to Emelye. "You get first dibs at the bath, of course. And then you can meet my lovely child. All of you, come come."

He offered Emelye his arm and they followed him through the town into his house. Despite the man's attire, the house was small. At least so Eramaus thought, until he realized it connected with the two houses next to it. One side was clearly the workshop and warehouse.

"Wait," Emelye stopped as they passed the crest over the door into the workshop. "Your, your Myron Psaki, crafter of all things fine and fair to grace your body and your hair?" Emelye turned to him.

His grin grew even wider. "I am indeed," he flourished a bow, "I see you are a cultured lass, but enough of that. To the baths!"

He led them through the opposite door and down a few steps to where a room was filled with steam. "I think you've got the baths good, Sauceda."

A tall, thin woman appeared through the fog. Eramaus blinked.

"She's Night." Emelye squeaked as she hopped back to grab Eramaus's arm.

The woman sighed and her gaze moved from her husband to Giles. "You didn't warn them, did you." It was more a statement than an accusation.

Giles gave a nervous chuckle. "Well, ah no, Tia, I forget."

"No matter." She looked back to Eramaus and Emelye. "Well, I see one of you has seen my kind before and had no-violent interactions."

"You, you speak Light so well," Emelye said as she peeled herself off Eramaus.

"Well, that's what happens when you are found in the Pass at a young age and taken in."

"Oh? Does that, does that happen frequently?"

The woman shrugged. "Don't know, but I can smell all four of you over the herbs." She pointed to Eramaus, "You go that way, there's a spare garment for you since I suspect you have no clean ones. And you," she smiled at Emelye, "this way. I have a spare garment for you too."

Eramaus headed to his bath, finding there was a partition around it. Sadly, it didn't keep out the thousand questions Emelye was peppering their host with. He dunked himself under as she began to talk of Thea, but when he came out there was silence.

Eramaus finished washing and quickly dressed in the kolobus he'd been given. It was a finer fabric than he'd expected. But if this was the maker of all those trinkets Lowri and the other princesses prized, he supposed the man would be well off.

Giles had given him directions to the dining hall before taking his bath. Emelye was there alone, staring out the window. "I didn't tell her about the Tower falling," she spoke softly as he stepped up beside her. "I, didn't want to have to tell that too many times, you know. She doesn't know about it. But she, she told me the Night have a prophecy like ours. She can't remember it, but she felt The Lady of Night tell her that this Lady of Light was the one."

Eramaus stood with her, gazing into the small courtyard that was shared with the houses behind this one.

"Heed the child of the Night, blessed by the Light, for she will guide you as our Gods reunite," Eramaus recited the last line of the prophecy Lady Katica had told them.

If Thea was the chosen one, then maybe Emelye was right. Maybe she was with the Night, learning from them, making friends among them. After all, here he was, in a home of the Light, with a woman of the Night.

⧢

Alethea sat in the darkness of a cave, though it was more a crevasse. She'd run across the log till an arrow hit her shoulder. And in some weird twist of fate, she'd fallen in here instead of to the churning water below. She knew her legs and arms were scrapped up. Her head hurt from where she'd whacked it on the low ceiling. But the arrow in her shoulder concerned her the most. Thankfully, it hadn't gone far in and she was able to pull it out.

Bandaging her wound as best she could with her wet clothing, she thought of the others. She knew she had a modicum of safety here, but did they? Not to mention she needed them. Despite how much she'd been learning, Alethea knew she was far from being able to look out for herself. Going back to Damadiosa was definitely not advisable, not that she had any provisions to even make that possible.

"Is there anyone I don't need to run from?" she sighed.

Your friends, the wind giggled as it played with the waterfall spray.

Alethea pursed her lips, her brows furrowing. "And where are my friends?"

About, was all she got.

"You are not helping!" Alethea directed her criticism to both The Lord and The Lady. "I can *NOT* bring these two, two, groups, together if they are both trying to kill me. I have no supplies to sustain me, and my friends are in enough danger that they *can't* help me!"

The wind sighed, a tendril of breeze gently caressing her cheek. *Rest*, it told her.

Exhaustion set in and Alethea managed to find a hollow in a rock to settle into before sleep overcame her. But sleep was not without unrest, as visions flashed behind her eyelids.

Juana bruised, one arm nearly useless, pulled herself from the water. Shadows danced across her vision as the sound shifted and returned to the waterfall's roar.

Toli beaten, curled into a whimpering mess, gently picked up by Tara. The shadows danced once more as the waterfall shifted its sound one way and then back.

Salina and Coleta nursed injuries, urging others toward a log. The one she'd crossed? Another shift.

This time, Alethea soared like a hawk, moving across the Pass to the north. Spiraling down, she watched a community, tucked in a valley hidden by the Dark Barrier. She was certain they were both Night and Light.

"Lady's Mother!"

Alethea started awake, her eyes drawn to the falling water. A person straddled on the log beyond it. They'd clearly slipped, but were unable to get back up, hampered by an arm hanging useless.

"Juana?" Alethea spoke as she rose.

The young woman continued her struggle as Alethea edged closer. Getting close to the beam meant getting close to the slippery edge, but she knew it had to be Juana.

"Lady's Mother and Matriarch!" Juana growled as her third attempt failed.

"Juana." Alethea reached out for the hurt arm. "Let me."

Juana's head spun that way, her body tensing before relaxing.

"Aletia?"

"Lady of Night, with your starlight," Alethea prayed, not waiting for consent, "let Juana's wounds be light, that she may help those who wish to sail with me into the sun. Enlighten-her." She let the soft starlight filter through her body, out her fingers, and onto Juana.

"Oh!" The girl let go, now suspended upside-down, only her legs keeping her on. She quickly righted herself, furrowing her brow. Alethea spoke before the girl could scold her for using 'Burnt Demon Sorcery'.

"The others went across the log. We should join them. I was given a vision of where we need to go." She spoke with more confidence than she felt, but she wanted to find the people she had seen.

Before Juana could question her, Alethea did her best to get onto the log. It was at waist height, the rock below it slippery. She slipped twice before Juana helped her. They moved slowly across the log this time. Focusing on the steps, Alethea managed to maintain balance on the slippery surface. It was so much easier when she wasn't running for her life.

The log ended, and she and Juana carefully transitioned to the next one, that switched back up the other way. Was this truly a secret path, like her path to the Holy Land? Did they need such a thing here? And how hidden was the entrance?

They transitioned a few more times, until the last log ended in the yawning maw of a cave. Alethea glanced back to Juana, who nodded. Swallowing, Alethea descended into darkness. She moved forward cautiously, giving Juana space. Juana didn't take the lead.

Closing her eyes, Alethea prayed. *All right Lord and Lady, a tiny bit of light and guidance would be greatly appreciated, Illumine and Enlighten-us.*

Juana gasped.

Opening her eyes, Alethea saw that she gave out a faint light. Better yet, there was a path of soft luminescence from the lichen on the wall.

Alethea led on as the tunnel twisted and turned. Occasionally it dipped down, but Alethea sensed it constantly went up. They heard the hushed whispers before they caught sight of firelight. Her luminescence faded and lichen light died as they approached. Juana crept ahead of her now, ready to fight as they listened.

"The Gran Mamara, is... dead?" Alethea recognized Coleta's shocked whisper.

"Even if she isn't," another voice spoke, "Lara is the leader by tradition."

"Tradition," a second voice joined in. "Lara spit on it the moment she used a newborn to claim her status."

"And yet you would follow Juana," Salina's voice cut in.

"Because she would have changed things the right way, and now she's dead too."

Alethea held Juana back, wanting to hear more, to be sure of these people.

"But why," the first unknown voice continued, "ally with, with, *that* woman? The families live in clans, the clans belong to tribes, and the tribes are all people of the Night, ruled by the council and led by the Gran Mamara. So why ally with an outcast and attack a gathering of the tribes."

"Tribes fight all the time," Coleta stated.

"But not at the Gran Fete," Salina pointed out. "Attacking at the Gran Fete is like declaring you want to fight all of the tribes."

"Lara spoke of change, and the new council members agreed," Coleta ruminated. "This was too big a change to be Aletia's fault." She sighed.

"It is." Alethea stepped past Juana and into the light. "And it isn't."

Standing just inside the light, Alethea surveyed all the people. Four campfires danced down the large cavern hall, at each one a family, or perhaps a clan. She was certain the shifts in the waterfall sound as she slept had been the sound of them crossing. Coleta sprung to her feet.

"Aletia! You are alive!"

Alethea winced as the woman squeezed her hard.

"So is Juana," Alethea gestured as the young woman stepped forward.

The crowd shifted, half of them standing. Coleta let Alethea go, allowing her to take a position behind Juana. These were Juana's people, after all. Alethea was still the outsider.

"Are you wounded?" Coleta asked.

"I was," Juana whispered, glancing back at Alethea.

Shivers ran down Alethea's spine as the chill of being soaked caught up to her. And others there shivered as well, even as they tried to stand proud and tall as Juana did. She caught Juana's gaze. So much had changed. Tradition had been broken, people had been divided, so why should she, Alethea, born of the Night, blessed by the Light, be bound by their rules. No! She gave Juana a slight smile that puzzled the woman. Alethea was going to do what was right.

Closing her eyes, she spread her arms wide, encompassing all of the people before her. Palms down, Alethea balled them into fists. "Lord, Lady," she spoke softly, "give us warmth and light to Illumine and enlighten us."

Motes of warmth filled her hands, until she could barely hold them. Turning her palms up, Alethea tossed them into the air. They flew, dancing and shimmering, raining upon the group. One settled on her nose, filling her with warmth. They all stared at her.

Alethea took a seat by Salina. The group about the fire stared with a mixture of shock, awe, and wariness. Her face flushed even as she smiled.

"Do all Light have this sorcery?" Coleta was the first to speak, plopping down on Alethea's other side. She'd caught her light mote in her hand and was looking at it so closely it almost touched her nose.

"No. I, um..." Alethea stopped trying to figure out what it was she wanted to say.

Juana stepped closer to them. "She was their equivalent of the Gran Mamara." Her eyes bore into Alethea.

"She has no children," Coleta stated.

"Was?" Salina queried.

Alethea gave a half smile, though she returned Jauna's gaze. "The Lady of Light is not supposed to have any children. But I am, I think, the youngest to have been anointed to that role. I should have had more years of training before Lady Katica," she swallowed, "passed away. But Lady Katica was one hundred and five."

Juana stoked the fire and Alethea turned to Salina. "As to the *was*, well, the people in power didn't like that I had been chosen. Things had been set up for another to take that role. One who looked more the part than I did. So they tried to kill me."

"But, why?" a man spoke, scooting closer.

Alethea recognized him as Maria's father.

"Because," Alethea sighed, "they couldn't see the Light in my Night, the way some people cannot see the Night in my Light."

Alethea gazed upward at the ceiling, wishing the Gran Mamara peace in her death, if she was dead.

"When a child of the Night," Juana spoke to the cavern, "becomes Lady of Light, old wounds she'll heal and try to make right. But when the lakes steam and the waters run dry, the end of the beginning is nigh. When you follow the chosen into the sun, know that our peoples will now be one."

Alethea felt everyone turn their attention to her.

"Why are we supposed to go into the sun?" a young voice piped up from another campfire.

Alethea smiled. "Well," she stood again, facing the crowd, "I keep asking The Lady of Night *and* The Lord of Light, but they both like to speak in riddles and dreams. But," she held up her hand as voices rose, "given the choices both the Light *and* the Night are making, I suspect this place will shake until it is swallowed by the sea."

"But that favors the Light, who can breathe underwater!" someone called out.

"Breath underwater?" Alethea's shock turned to laughter and she took a quick breath to stop it. "The Light can't breathe underwater," she responded seriously, "any more than the Night can fly."

"They can't?" the young one piped up again.

"As far as I know. I don't even know how to swim, let alone breathe water," Alethea stated. She looked about the group at her fire. "And the Night can't fly, right?"

"Some of us have gliders, but fly like a bird," Salina shook her head, "no."

"See, you use a tool like the Light, for they have ~boats~ that move on the top of the water." And, she thought, not wanting to disturb things more, they were going to need boats, and sailors that wouldn't toss any Night overboard at the first whiff of a storm.

ৰୠ

Juana spoke quietly to the eldest of the women there. Alethea couldn't hear what they spoke about, but she felt all of them continually glancing at her. She hoped it wasn't a discussion about letting her stay or not, though the glances did not feel hostile, only curious. Finally there was an agreement of some sort and Juana came to Alethea.

"Our new council has decided you should join us."

"Me? But I—" she began.

But Juana cut her off. "Lara has broken all tradition, and there is no sense for us to continue with it. You and I will be part of the council, though we do not have children." Juana's gaze flicked to the group she'd been talking with. "Will you join us?"

Alethea nodded consent and she and Juana joined the others. The women filled them in on their discussion about the futility of retaking Damadiosa. Juana agreed, as did Alethea. Afterall, that would be counter to finding the people she'd seen. Not that she had any idea of how to convince these women to follow her lead.

"Could this place be found?" Alethea asked, suddenly concerned.

Juana shook her head. "The Gran Mamara," she paused for a moment, "told me of it, only just before The Games. And I told only those whom I trusted, and whom are here." Her head hung for a moment and Alethea barely caught her whispered, "Expect Toli."

It was clear, however, and they all agreed, they couldn't stay there. Their sudden departure meant there was little food, though the men did what they could with what they had taken from the feasts. Alethea blessed it, as she had the food on her journey to Archtheos. How long ago had that been? It felt like yesterday, but also years ago, though it had only been a few months. She'd been different then.

Unfortunately, they also agreed that they needed to stay there a little bit longer to avoid being captured upon emerging. Sitting idle, however, was not conducive to a cooperative mood. It wasn't long before people began to bicker. Alethea did as she could to ignore the growing chaos, until a new person showed up.

Coleta was first to call out, barring the person's path. Juana and Salina were not far behind with the other warriors. Alethea ignored it until the person spoke.

"Please?" Tara spoke. "Toli's dying. Kill me if you must, but help him. Please?"

"Fine with me," Coleta growled as the women crowded forward.

"Wait!" Alethea commanded, pushing her way to the front. "Wait," she spoke once more as she stood before Tara, who was holding a battered Toli.

"Aletia," Juana began, but her voice fell silent as Toli coughed blood.

Tara's gaze shifted from Juana to Alethea. The girl had bruises on her face, arms, and legs, but Toli was worse. One eye was totally swollen shut. His breath came in shallow gasps that made him grimace. Not to mention that both legs looked broken. Tara regarded Alethea with tears running down her mud streaked face.

"Please, use, use, your Light sorcery and heal him. Please? He's in pain, he's dying. I never wanted him to die," she sobbed out the last word.

"Juana," Alethea ordered, "take him, gently, and lay him on a bedroll as soft as you can." Juana nodded. "Coleta and Salina, guard Tara. Be kind," she spoke firmly. "She is bruised, and I want her to remain here and *un*harmed." The last word she said to the gathered crowd.

As Tara surrendered herself to Coleta's hold, her eyes looked up to Alethea. "You will mend him?"

"I will ~heal~ him," she told the girl, "because it is the right thing to do. As it was right for you to bring him here."

Tara bowed her head.

Alethea moved herself from the group that now surrounded Tara and knelt beside Toli. She noticed the men had crept closer.

"Women mend among the Light?" one of them asked as she held her hands over Toli.

The damage was extensive. Tara was right, he was dying. She took a deep breath as she set her resolve to do what needed to be done.

"Yes," she responded, glancing to the speaker. "Women, who are like your poporos, learn to mend, what we call ~heal~." She looked at those who had gathered in, children and a few young women among them. "What I do, is, different. I pray, and the Gods listen." She blinked and turned back to Toli. "But even with their help, it takes much of my energy, so I may pass out and will need food when I wake."

Maria's father nodded in understanding. Alethea raised her eyes to the roof of the cavern. Even in darkness there is light. Taking a deep breath Alethea closed her eyes. She pictured the brightest moonlit night she could and fairest sunny day.

"Lady of Night and Lord of Light," she prayed, "lend me your gift of healing so that I may bestow it upon Toli, your humble servant, to heal him, that he may continue with me to fight for what is right as our two peoples unite. Enlighten and Illumine-him."

She spread her arms wide, reaching them up and out. She felt, more than saw, the walls began to glow, silver and gold intertwining. It poured into her like the warmest mountain day and the coolest coastal night. It gathered and pooled about her, bubbled up from inside her. Opening her eyes, she brought her hands down to direct the light to Toli's ribs, and his legs, and all the bruises. A gentle laughter filled the air as it spilled out over Toli, reaching out to all who sat in the cavern.

"Be blessed, my children of the stars, for she is one of you as much as she is one of them," it whispered like the wind through reeds and silence settled about them.

The light faded into darkness, and Alethea was present enough to make sure she didn't fall on Toli.

When she woke, Tara and Toli were softly arguing. Alethea sat up and they went silent. Most of the fires had died down, and the cavern was filled with the sound of gentle breathing. Toli handed Alethea the food that had been kept warm for her. She took it gratefully and tried to judge what was going on between them. Toli nudged at Tara, who was bound tight. Tara's brows furrowed, but she didn't say anything until Alethea finished eating.

"I should go back," Tara stated. "They've stopped looking for you, but if I stay longer, they will think something is up."

"Can you go back without Toli?" Alethea asked.

Tara swallowed and bowed her head. "I was sent out to kill him," she swallowed, "so yes."

"The others won't let her leave, not even Juana." Toli leaned forward. "I told her she should let me free her and sneak out, but she won't."

Alethea studied Tara. The girl hesitantly lifted her eyes to meet Alethea's. "She wanted me to kill my brother, my *twin* brother. I swear, if you promise to keep him safe, I promise I will give *nothing*, absolutely *nothing* away. I will even break the logs, so they cannot use them to get to you. Please, I swear upon, upon my life, The Lady, *and* The Lord."

Her voice burned with a sibling's passion for the brother she'd been born with. Alethea felt the love of the twin's bond between them.

"Tara," Alethea reached out, taking Tara's bound hands in her own, "I promise that Toli will remain with us. And so long as we are safe, he is safe. Do you understand?"

Tara nodded her head, tears filling the corners of her eyes.

Alethea unbound her.

"HEY!" Coleta jolted from her doze as Tara stepped over her.

Alethea touched the big woman's leg. "Let her go," she said as Juana rose, spear poised. "So long as we protect Toli, she will protect us. The Lord *and* The Lady believe in her love of him, as do I."

Chapter 15

∽⟫⟨∾

They waited for four days before Anchises showed up. What Eramaus didn't expect was Anchises showing up at dinner time and greeting Myron as a good friend. He and Emelye waited with Giles and Basil in a back room as Myron and his wife exchanged pleasantries. Then there was apparently business.

"I mean, it makes sense that Myron would be commissioned to create a piece for the wedding." Emelye sighed. "Frankly, I'm surprised Lowri didn't have it commissioned the day she left for Archtheos."

"Probably before." Eramaus echoed her sigh as he paced the room. He stopped the moment his knight mentor paused in the doorway.

Anchises glanced from Eramaus to Emelye and then to Basil and Giles. Silence settled about them as he stepped into the room with Myron. Eramaus was certain the man would berate him for leaving his post at any moment. After all, he'd been entrusted with the key to the Tower, entrusted to guard Lyrcus.

"I sense," Anchises broke the silence at last, "there is more to tell than what has been told. And there is truth to the rumors I have heard on the streets."

Emelye pushed Eramaus forward, but, before he could speak, Sauceda entered with drinks. She was followed by Diono, their morose child. Eramaus couldn't figure out if Diono was a boy or a girl, and Myron and Sauceda didn't make it any clearer. He wondered if the kid even wanted to get married.

Sauceda made them all sit and sip their drink before she turned to Eramaus. "I hear this is your story to tell."

Eramaus swallowed as all eyes turned to him. It was hard to get the words out, hard to tell where to start. But with encouragement, and the occasional righteous outburst from Emelye, he managed to tell how he'd been assigned to Prince Lyrcus. How he'd visited Thea that day with said prince, only to turn around and sprint back to the Tower as it was attacked. Yet when he got there, calling her name, his body went limp.

"He went mad," Emelye interjected. "Well you did," she muttered as Eramaus glared at her, "laughing maniacally as the Tower fell."

"It fell?" Anchises leaned forward, shock finally showing on his face.

Eramaus told him how it fell with the quaking of the earth. And how he and other prisoners had been forced to dig bodies out of the rubble, while Emelye was made to tend to those who might survive.

"Vile people, every one of them," she muttered.

"And they let you go?" Anchises asked, "with no..." his eyes glanced to their right wrists.

Eramaus rubbed his. "Well..." he looked to his cousin.

She took up the tale from there, recounting how Captain Boreas had taken them in, but he was working on the proper documentation when there was another quake. "And he," she thumbed at Eramaus, "just called out to The Lord of Light, and next thing I know, our bracelets just popped off."

Anchises smiled, for the first time since listening. "You are blessed, Eramaus. The Lord has a plan for you, even if you do not wish to see it." He sighed and stood. "Anything else that I should know before I go? I have been here almost too long."

Emelye quickly spouted off that Daphne was now going to be Lady of Light and Lowri the new Empress. And that *she* suspected Lowri was behind the Emperor's death since she didn't want anyone stealing her glory the way she thought Alethea had.

Eramaus snorted, but Anchises looked at him and Emelye again. "And do you think our Lady of Light still lives?"

"Absolutely." Emelye emphatically nodded.

Eramaus took in a slow breath as Anchises turned to him. "If, if she does," he met the knight's gaze, "she would be with the Night. And if, if she is," the words were hard to get out, like saying them gave him hope he shouldn't have, "I know, she has, friends, at least, at least three."

He could feel Emelye's glare and knew she was about to say something, argue with him about this fact. But Anchises gave her a look that quelled her ire before nodding to them all.

"I hope to see you all in Paramythia. I suspect there are many changes happening that will keep me there for a while."

∾∾

"I'm staying," Emelye announced as they got ready to leave the next day.

"What?" Eramaus blinked at her, taking a slight step back from his cousin. She gave Giles and Basil a farewell arm grip before turning to him as those two walked off a little ways.

"Are you sure, Em? I mean, I don't see you marrying Diono."

"Oh I'm not," Emelye laughed. "But I'm not cut out to be a mercenary, either. You all are too gross." She waved a hand at him and the other two as if to dismiss them.

"But," Eramaus looked at his cousin, feeling as if the last of his family was leaving him alone. Thea gone, now "Em?" He swallowed.

"Oh, Eramaus!" Emelye hugged him tightly. "Look, you're a thick-headed, stubborn, old boar, but you are family." She let him go. "And I *will*," she poked him in the chest, "see you again. I'm just needed here and feel quite welcome to stay."

Eramaus frowned at her.

"I'm serious, Eramaus."

He sighed.

"No," she poked his chest, "you will *not* mope, and you *will* find Alethea. Do you understand me?"

"What if she doesn't want to be found, Em? They tried to kill her."

Em barked a laugh. "You told me a while ago you'd go above the Dead Zone to be with her. Don't tell me *that's* changed."

"But I didn't do as she asked me to. I'm not..." All of his doubts crashed into his throat, leaving him silent.

"Eramaus Spanos, if I could smack sense into that skull of yours, I would. *I* can only love Alethea from afar. You are the one *she* loves. And if you still love her, then she *definitely* still loves you. Now go!" Emelye forced him around and shoved him toward Giles and Basil. "And be sure to visit your mother!" she called after him before going into the house.

Swallowing with another breath, Eramaus plodded over to the other two. They gave him a thump on the back before setting a brisk pace.

The road between Smyria and Valaora was nearly as unpopulated as the one between Smyria and Gorgomilos. There was a way station, but Eramaus kept them going, knowing his father's summer house—where his mother ought to be staying—wasn't much further off. It was the first of the manors that sprung up along this road once it came within sight of the sea.

The front gate was, of course, closed, and Eramaus didn't feel like pulling the rope to ring the bell. The fewer people who knew he was there the better. Even if Lowri, or Poulos, wasn't looking for him, it just felt safer. Basil and Giles didn't question it as he led them through the jungle around to the back of the manor house.

He was surprised to see Ada Mos waiting at the gate. She opened it, letting them in, whispering quiet words to Basil and Giles, who nodded and headed to the stables. Eramaus stayed there, looking into the courtyard and then down the path. It felt like it had been years ago when he'd seen Thea here for the first time in five years and they had walked down that path. He remembered how the Count had refused his proposal to marry her, and how, if that happened now, he wouldn't take no for an answer. He sighed.

"Aye, we miss her too."

Eramaus glanced at Ada Mos.

"Go. I'll leave the gate unlocked and make sure Giles and Basil save you some supper."

❧❧

Eramaus walked the path, his hands trailing along the leaves. He shouldn't be out so late. He was hungry and tired. But this place whispered of the past to him, pulling him to the shore. Here he faced his shortcomings. Yet it whispered of hope.

He let the waves lap his toes, wondering if he could just walk into the water to be no more, to disappear. He remembered the night he tried to bash his head on the Dead Zone.

The wind would not let him then, and the waves whispered to him now. It was not his time, he still had work to do.

Heaving a sign, Eramaus hurried back to the gate. He jolted to a stop just as the gate came into view. Two figures stood by it, whispering in the soft tones of lovers. One he was certain was his mother's. The other...

"Count Manella?"

The words left his mouth before he could stop them. He stepped toward the couple, showing himself in the moonlight. He looked between them. Oh, they were lovers. They were lovers for sure. He felt his blood run cold, his hand gripping his sword.

"How long?" he hissed.

"Eramaus, please." His mother spoke, and when his eyes swiveled to her, she shivered.

"How long, *Mother?*"

"Since before you were born, Sofi asked—" the words stammered out.

"Sofi asked?" Incredulousness colored his voice. "You slept with your best friend's husband because she asked?"

Eramaus remembered how devastated his mother had been at Sofi's death. And yet, this was also how she...

No wonder he'd spent so many summers here after Sofi's death. *Alethea needed a friend, Alethea needed...* If they'd have thought about what Alethea needed, it wouldn't have been him. All he had done was lead her into trouble.

"You were supposed to be hers."

Eramaus blinked. "What?"

"The, the Count, he's your father. Not the Duke."

"What?" The words coming out of her mouth made no sense to him.

"Stephana, I am not sure if we should be talking to him right now, he is—,"

"I am what?" Eramaus turned and stepped toward him.

"In league with the false Lady who *you* once considered your daughter? Maybe you should have let me marry her."

"She's a Shadow Fiend, I—"

"Is that how you feel," Eramaus stepped forward again, making the count step back, "about the child that gave your wife joy? About the young woman anointed Lady of Light, by THE LORD, Himself? Alethea may be half Night, but she is *ALL* Light." Eramaus forced himself to loose his grip on his sword and step back. "But you kept Thea from harm until she was thrown into *that* feline den, so I won't skewer you, for her sake."

"Eramaus!"

Eramaus looked to his horrified mother's face. "Mother, you have not seen what people have said of her. You know Thea as well as *he* should," he gestured to the Count. "When has she *ever* seemed to want to fight anyone, or take control, or displayed any trait we attribute to the Night?"

His mother hung her head. "Never," she whispered. "Which is why—"

"Exactly." He glared at them both. "And I've fought the Night. Spoken to one outside of combat. They are no more wrong than we are right!" Warmth filled him. *Right not Might* echoed in his brain.

He brushed past the count to the gate. "I did not come to argue," he sighed and turned back to them. "I came to ask for shelter, and speak with you, mother. I just," he studied them both, "I need the truth. I need to know that I won't be betrayed." His eyes flicked at the Count. "By you or any others in this household."

His hand glowed and he turned his palm up to see a small ball of golden light. He flicked some at his mother, and more at the Count, and the rest toward the servant's quarters.

"Truth," he stated.

"No one will betray you," his mother stated with a confidence he rarely saw in her. She turned to the Count. "But we will need more supplies if you plan to stay."

The Count made a face. Clearly, he was the one doing the provisioning. How could he hate the Night so much that he was so clouded against the girl that grew up under his care. When did he figure it out? When Sofi came home with a child that was happy and healthy? And, it hit him, he probably did love Alethea till Sofi died. The count had seen only the Light in the child until then, but his heart had broken. Eramaus knew what that was like. Could almost pity the Count for blaming Alethea for Sofi's death.

"Thank you." He nodded to them both, then turned to leave so they could have their lovers' good-bye.

Basil and Giles were already snoring in the loft. Eramaus ate the food they had left, but restlessness still plagued him, and he found himself at the house chapel. Stopping inside, he stared at the symbol of The Lord as it glowed in the pale moonlight. The door opened, and he could tell by the soft footsteps it was his mother. She stopped next to him.

"He, he is your real father, you know."

"The Count?" Eramaus tried not to spit the man's name. By the fare Ada Mos had given, he could tell Count Manella had been keeping her supplied, well beyond what he knew his father would have paid for.

"Yes," she paused slightly. "Sofi and I were hoping if we became pregnant at the same time, and she carried close to term, we could 'give birth' together. I could give her my healthy child, since all my children survived, and I would take the sickly one. But she wasn't able to carry that one to term. And the Duke decided I should stop visiting her until I'd given birth lest I lose my child as well." She sighed and placed her hand on his arm. "I'm sorry, Eramaus. I should have given you to Sofi. You should have been raised as the Count's son."

Eramaus remained silent in his thoughts until his mother

left. He glanced at her retreating form then back to the stained-glass window. In some other life, some other version of themselves, he would have been a Merchant's son, and fallen in love with a Captain's niece. But here he was, stuck in the middle of a conflict that shouldn't be. Heaving a sigh, he turned with one glance backward before exiting.

"Illumine-me Lord, for I'm going to need all the guidance I can get."

His hair was ruffled by a loving breeze and he finally felt ready for sleep.

Chapter 16

When Eramaus's mother made a fuss over him the next day, he grumbled that they needed to leave.

"Leave, but you just got here. I didn't think I'd get to see you again until you were doing rounds and—" she stopped, looking at Giles and Basil, then leaned into him whispering, "—they aren't squires are they?"

"No," Eramaus hung his head. "They are mercenaries with Captain Boreas."

"But," she placed a finger under his chin so she could tilt his face to hers, "you are still a squire, aren't you?"

Eramaus shot an apologetic glance to the mercenaries at the side gate. Basil nodded in understanding, while Giles gave sympathetic smile. Both waved and headed off, letting Eramaus focus on his mother.

"You haven't heard, have you?"

"Danaus brings me news. This place is designed to be self-sufficient for the most part. And the Duke isn't giving me much in the way of a travel allowance."

"Then either the news hasn't reached Count Manella, or

he's not telling you things."

"Why wouldn't he tell me things?"

Eramaus bit his lip, then guided his mother through the gate to the waterfall. How often had he come there with Thea. His throat tried to close, and he swallowed.

"Eramaus," her hand rubbed his back as it often had when he was little and upset. "What happened? Alethea is still Lady of Light, is she not? Emelye, she's still a mediki, yes?"

Eramaus shook his head, struggling through the emotions that tightened his chest. He turned to his mother, taking both her hands in his own.

"The Tower of Light fell."

"Fell? But it's…"

"They attacked it." Eramaus swallowed the lump in his throat.

"Attacked the Tower of Light?" Her eyes went wide. "Why would they do such a thing?"

"Mother, you, you heard what Manella called her."

"I took him to task for that, you can believe me."

"Well, he wasn't the only one who thought she was all, all, shadow fiend." The words came out as hateful things. He hated to say it, not after learning she was part Night and Light.

"But, she's not. Like you told Danaus last night. She's pure light, her looks, I mean," His mother floundered, sitting down on the closest rock. "Oh I tried to keep her from the Holy City. I would have taken her there on pilgrimage once I knew the Holy Land was open, but oh, she wanted to be a mediki and Danaus didn't want to see her again. She reminded him too much of Sofi, so he didn't even try to dissuade her of that. But I knew she had so much Light, she ought to be protected. I should have done more to persuade her to be my maid in waiting. I could have kept her safe and," Her hand flew from him to her face as she wailed.

Eramaus had never seen his mother sob so fiercely in his

life. He couldn't tell if the tapestry of his life was unraveling, or being...

Woven.

He was learning new things. Things he'd never have thought to even ask about. They filled in the holes of a tapestry he'd barely noticed. His mother had wanted to protect Thea, too. And he should do something, give her the same hope Emelye had been trying to give him.

Dropping to his knees, Eramaus gently took his mother's hands from her face. He squeezed them. "Mother. Please, look at me."

Her face lifted slightly, and he was able to catch her eyes. "I," his brows furrowed. What did he want to say? "I don't think anything would have changed had you persuaded Alethea to be your maid in waiting."

Stephana heaved a sob, her breath quivering. "I knew it, the moment you decided to go with her. I knew she would become Lady of Light. You, you," she freed a hand to wipe the tears that had snuck onto his cheek, "should become a Knight and then the Paladin with her. You have that bond with her, don't you."

Eramaus blinked, his face turning to the sky. "First Thea tells me You'd prefer me as a Knight, now my mother echoes Anchises, saying I should become Paladin because I love her? Seriously, Lord?"

"You love her?" His mother rose, bringing Eramaus with her.

He looked back to his mother with a chagrined smile. "As painful as it has been, yes, I do. And I sense there's still things I need to do before I see her again."

"But, you said they attacked the Tower, and it fell?" Tears welled up in her eyes, threatening to spill over again.

Eramaus sighed. He wanted to leave now, get back to Paramythia. Maybe The Lord wasn't talking to him right now, but that didn't mean he could stand still. Thea had charged him with keeping Lyrcus safe, and he needed to figure out how to do that.

"Eramaus?" His mother's plaintive question centered his spinning brain.

He blinked and focused on his mother as he spoke to her of all the things that had transpired. From the attempts on Alethea's life, though he glossed over the stabbing, to the final attack on the Tower. He spoke of how he and Emelye had been thrown in prison, forced to help with the Tower excavation, how Captain Boreas had taken them in, and how Emelye had stayed behind in Smyria.

His mother nodded, not asking a single question. When he was done, she gazed thoughtfully at him, tears still shining in her eyes. Her embrace was warm and comforting, filled with love. *All Love*, the wind whispered about him as his mother kissed both his cheeks before stepping back.

"Go, do what The Lord asks of you and be with Alethea." She smiled, her hands forming the symbol of the Bleeding Hearts resting on her chest. "There are things I must do and people to collect."

Eramaus furrowed his brows, blinking rapidly. She patted his shoulder then fluttered her hands at him before turning and marching back into the house.

With a shake of his head, Eramaus made his way round the manor to the road to Valaora. It was only a half day's walk, and he took it slow. There was plenty of time to reach the gates before they closed, though his stomach did protest that he hadn't thought to grab food. Eramaus sighed, Emelye would have remembered

Downright starving by the time he got to Seneca Tavern, he plopped down next to Basil and reached in for the food.

"Pay up." Basil grinned as the crew greeted him. "I told ya that posh livin' ain't for him and he'd be back."

There were some good natured grumbles as coins were handed to Basil, who then split them with Giles. The Captain sat down at the table and shook his head.

"Good visit with ye mum?"

Eramaus nodded, his mouth full of food. It felt good to be with these men. More at home, though he'd always be that duke's son, even though he wasn't. He was a count's son.

He lingered in the tavern, nursing his drink as everyone went to their beds. The Captain moved to sit beside him once they were the only two left.

"No one told her, my mother, of the Tower. And I didn't think to tell her of the rest."

"I'm sure she knows of the Emperor's passing. But I think they be keeping the secret of the Tower to themselves. How'd yer mum take it?"

"Worse than expected, but also well." He stared at Boreas, whispering, "she's a Bleeding Heart."

"Aye, she feels more than most people do. That's why she's in this debacle with tha Count."

Eramaus furrowed his brow. "Don't tell me you knew who *my* parents really are too."

Grinning, Boreas winked. "Get some sleep lad. We got wagons ta load in tha mornin'."

₽ъↆ

Everyone but Toli was displeased that Alethea let Tara go.

"It was the *right* thing to do," she insisted. "We keep Toli safe. She keeps us safe."

Juana snorted. The rest of the council frowned. They quickly decided it was time to leave, and called for the men to pack. Alethea helped as best she could and made no complaint about what she was given to carry. They moved single file down the tunnel. Looking back, Alethea saw that the whole thing was a tunnel, they had just camped at its widest spot. At one point, they had to shed their packs and pass them through a narrow opening. Coleta got stuck and it took a little pushing, pulling, and a tiny prayer to get her through. They came out to rain.

"It'll hide the tracks," Salina stated softly as they continued, trying best to step in each other's footprints.

Juana led, keeping them moving, and only allowing them rest at the peak of the day and deep of night. By the second evening, the group was fully in the shadow of Palos peak. They were so close they could feel heat emanating from the ground. The smoke drifting down the slope tweaked their noses with the smell of rotten eggs.

Alethea caught Juana after she had directed two small groups to go hunting. "We need to go toward the ~Pass~, where the Light cross."

Juana frowned. "The outcasts live near the Burnt Valley. It is better to avoid them." She turned away.

Alethea reached for Juana's shoulder. "Juana." She gripped the young woman as Juana turned to her, clearly annoyed. "Are all outcasts like Brisa?"

Juana shook her head.

"And if Lara is in charge with Brisa backing her, are *we* not the outcasts, now?" Alethea dropped her arm, watching realization slowly cross Juana's face. "And," Alethea took a deep breath. "Do you not believe that I am the one chosen to lead us into the sun?"

"Yes, but," Juana stopped her face flashing multiple emotions, grief the most prominent.

Gently guiding Juana, Alethea moved them away from where Toli and the other men were making their evening camp. They stopped on an outcropping of rock and stood surveying the land around them. The light was fading, the sun setting just behind their periphery.

"You have lost someone close to you without being able to say goodbye," Alethea spoke softly, gently wrapping her arm about the young girl's shoulder. "I understand."

Juana threw off her arm and turned on her. "Do you? Who have you lost? A woman to old age, a…"

Her rage was palpable. Alethea resisted stepping back, instead she stepped forward.

"Who have I lost?"

"Yes," Juana stepped closer so that they were nose to nose. "Who *have* you lost?"

"The birth parents I can't remember." Alethea began to tick them off one by one. "At *five* the mother who sang me to sleep. Not long ago, Lady Katica, who had just begun to teach me, followed quickly by the man who was protecting me. And sure, you can say she died of old age and he of heartbreak, but I'm certain ~poison~ was involved." She kept her eyes locked on Juana's. "And why don't we count how I made friends but had to leave them behind to The Lord and The Lady only knows what fate. And even if they aren't dead, they might as well be with how far I am from reuniting with them!"

She breathed heavily, surprised at the warmth running through her veins. There was a strength in anger, but it needed channeling.

"And," she softened her voice, "we are going to lose more. There are not enough ~boats~ and people to save everyone. Not enough who will believe they must leave, let alone be willing to share space with those who are not like them. But," a soft smile crept onto her face, "we also gain people. I've gained you, and Toli, and Coleta, and Salina."

Alethea wrapped her arms around Juana as Emelye would do to her. She pulled Juana into a fierce hug. Juana stood stiff and Alethea felt the anger, but she held the embrace until Juana softened.

"Mamara Mari, she, she knew what to say," Juana's voice

broke. "Knew what to do. I was still training. I, I can lead the women in a fight, I can lead them in the hunt, but where to go and what to do? I don't know how to do that. How do you know?"

She pulled back and Alethea let her. Silent tears slowly meandered down Juana's cheeks. Alethea took Juana's hand in her own as she caught Juana's gaze.

"How do you know," Juana asked, "that toward the Burnt Valley is where we need to go? What good will that do us? How will we get off this peak and out, to," she pulled a hand free, gesturing wildly to the land before them, "to wherever it is you are to lead us to?"

Alethea glanced to the sky where the first bright star of the night blinked into existence. "I pray for guidance."

"And you said you only get riddles," Juana countered.

"Yes," she looked back to Juana, "but I also know that Love is the binding thread for what I must do. You love these people you are leading, do you not?"

"Not like that!" Juana began.

Raising a hand, Alethea quieted her. "There are many types of love, Juana. Tara loves her brother more than her own life, as you loved the Gran Mamara as one would a mother. Coleta and Salina have a love that is like siblings, though they are not. Is none of that true?"

Juana studied Alethea for a moment, pondering. She shook her head. "It's true," she whispered.

"The night I healed you," Alethea continued, "I was given a vision in which I saw a village of people, Night and Light, living in harmony. I think they will be key in gathering all those who *do* believe in Love, All Love, together before we ~sail across the sea~."

A puzzled look crossed Juana's face, as she tried to understand the words in Light.

"Follow me into the sun." Alethea smiled softly as she

pulled Juana in for another hug. This time Juana hugged back, her quiet tears rolling onto Alethea's shoulder. When the girl's grip relaxed a little, Alethea gave her an extra squeeze before letting her go. A smile peeked through Juana's grief. Squeezing Juana's shoulder, Alethea headed back to camp, letting Juana regain her composure in quiet solitude.

☙◊❧

Juana kept them off any worn trails the next day, making for labored walking. They were not far from the Pass now and an odd familiarity tugged at Alethea's mind. Stepping forward, she cried out as the ground buckled under her. Falling backward, her feet skipping into the air, Alethea's butt hit the ground as it rolled like the ocean. She landed on leaves and slid down a steep bank, the ground rocking and shaking, tossing her one way then another. Then it stopped.

Laying on the ground, Alethea stared up. This was not the Pass, where she'd expected to be taken. Trees crowded over this place like a protective canopy. Familiarity washed over her like a wave. Narrowing her eyes, she un-focused them. Why did she know this place?

"Aletia?" Coleta's voice called the hill.

"Down here," Alethea responded, slowly standing.

She didn't feel hurt, though she was certain her butt would be sore in the morning. Turning to face the way she'd come, she saw Coleta half skipping half sliding her way. Alethea chuckled as she moved out of the way before the big girl crashed into her.

Coleta grabbed a tree, using it to pivot back to Alethea. "You all right?"

"Fine," Alethea said as she continued to gaze about her.

The draw of a familiarity pulled Alethea to move past Coleta. Her hands brushed the leaves of a willow tree. It had been smaller. She blinked and moved forward parting the branches to move beyond it.

"Coleta, bring Aletia up here, we need to find shelter. There's injuries."

"There's shelter here," Alethea called back before Coleta could answer.

She stared into the mouth of a cave. She heard Coleta approach, but didn't turn.

"Huh, so there is," Coleta stated. "Stay here, I'll get the others down."

Alethea nodded as she absently began to slowly turn around. Echoes of a babe's laughter and parental voices taunted her senses. She almost saw them, a woman with bow and spear, a man with a sword, a babe between them. She stepped away from the cave as if she could move closer and see them clearer.

"Aletia," Juana's voice broke the vision.

Blinking, Alethea turned to see a young woman gesture to those being helped down the hill. Nodding, Alethea moved forward to bless each one and quicken their healing. Salina was the last down, hobbling with help from a stout stick. She waved off Alethea's blessing as Toli called out.

"This cave's been used."

Everyone turned their attention to him.

"When?" Juana asked. "Because I don't want to be surprised down here."

"Oh, not for a while," Toli said as he continued to clear debris from a ring of stones just inside the cave entrance.

"Saves us work." Maria's father smiled as he dropped a load of sticks next to it.

Alethea stared at it curiously before regarding the cave again. Laughter echoed back at her. "Lady of Night give me a little light," Alethea whispered, gathering dappled sunlight in her hands, "Enlighten-me." She threw it above her head and it floated there, softly illuminating around her.

"That's a neat trick," Salina spoke from beside her, "but what are you going to do with it?"

"Explore the cave." Alethea took a step inside.

"It's a cave," Salina stated, "and there will be torches soon enough."

"Yes," Alethea stepped into the dim interior, "but I know this place."

Chapter 17

The floor of the cave was littered with leaves and decomposed matter. None of that struck any memories. Alethea moved further back, her light shining softly on the walls and floor. The familiarity lingered so tantalizingly close. She was deep in, where the entrance light barely reached, yet a tiny spot of light shone down from a hole in the roof. Below it was another ring of stones, filled with the dirt of decomposed logs. Alethea knelt by it.

A man held her chubby baby hands, which grasped a stick, burnt on one end. He guided her hand in making letters on the floor. She giggled. A woman laughed.

"What is she going to do with those, Claus?"

"Hey, maybe she will need to converse with the Light one day. Best she knows both, Zoraida."

He guided her hand in an A, L, T, H, E, A.

"What does that mean?" Salina's voice broke the vision. Alethea blinked. She looked to her hand which had drawn the letters as if the vision had been real.

"My name," she whispered.

"Aletia?"

"Althea," she answered, still staring at it. "Not Alethea," she half whispered.

Standing, Alethea brushed off her knees. Slowly she turned to face the opposite wall. The debris was piled higher there. Alethea walked over to it, almost in a daze.

Now a woman guided Alethea's fingers, dipped in a concoction of berry juice and ash from the fire. She knelt on the bed, while Althea stood.

"One stroke for the ground."

And her childish hand painted the wall.

The man chuckled, "What is she going to do with those, Zoraida."

"You never know if she needs to interact with the Night someday, Claus," the woman laughed back.

Alethea knelt and placed a hand on the place where a bed was—had been—years ago now. She brushed away dirt from the wall and waved her light forward to shine on it. The childish drawings remained. Salina gasped slightly as she knelt next to Alethea.

"Sunrise," Salina's hand traced the design in the air, "and sunset." Her gaze shifted to Alethea. "How did you know they'd be there? Do you think there are others?"

Alethea stood, throwing her light up to the ceiling, where it diffused, shedding dim light about the whole space. It wasn't that big, really. An inner hearth and outer hearth, a bed area, and a living space, where they might have waited out the rain.

"TOLI!" Coleta yelled, voice quavering. "I need a poporo!"

Alethea turned, the sound of a phantom fight in her ears. She hurried over with Toli, Salina hobbling after. Coleta held out a bone, her arm shaking.

Toli took it from her. "Lady of Night, forgive Coleta, for she knew not what she touched. Enlighten-us." Toli's free arm reached out to touch Coleta and she sighed, fear draining from her.

"I tripped over something, and I reached down to pick it up and toss it so it wouldn't trip anyone else, and, well um," she gestured wildly at the bone Toli now held.

He nodded. "I'll cleanse the area and ensure the soul is released."

"I'll help." Alethea began to kneel.

There was an intake of breath. And she glanced at those around her.

"Only poporos may touch the dead and dying," Coleta stated.

They all looked at her, wary.

Alethea sighed. "Among the Light," she told them, "anyone might touch the dead." Alethea gave a soft smile. "Though only a trained ~mediki~, who are like your poporos, may prepare the dead for burial."

"And you are trained?" Toli asked, looking up from where he was gently uncovering the bones.

"Yes." She knelt down next to him and began to help. "I have performed the ~rite~ two times." She looked up at the still shocked faces about her. "If we are living in the time of the prophecy, we cannot think in terms of the Night or the Light, but rather what we feel is right."

She placed a hand to her heart, closing her eyes as she formed the Bleeding Heart symbol. Opening her eyes, she returned to brushing away dirt from the skeleton. She paused, picking up a bronze broach, a red coral teardrop set in it. She glanced to Toli who looked at her curiously.

"I, I think this was my true father."

෪෨

That evening, Alethea helped Toli mend those who had been injured. Or rather, he mended, and she blessed them with quicker healing. As the sun set behind the gray clouds, Alethea stood before the grave she and Toli had made for the bones Coleta had stumbled across. She fingered the broach, which Salina had cleaned off for her after Toli cleansed it with a prayer. It reminded her of Eramaus, of the Bleeding Hearts, and how they had guarded her in Archtheos. Rubbing her thumb over the polished surface she wondered how she had ended up at Count Danella's.

Toli suspected there had been a fight. He'd found an obsidian spearhead buried in one shoulder. It had shattered the coral in the second broach. He'd also indicated the cracks in the skeleton's skull were like those he'd tended before, made by a long staff. The body's proportions, they agreed, were more Light than Night. This was also supported by the squire's broach and the nearby broken and rusted sword.

"Are you my true father?" Alethea asked softly. "Did you fight so my mother could run with me? Is that why we haven't found her bones? Is that why I'm alive?" She blinked back tears. "She didn't make it, not that I remember. But I'm sure The Lord and The Lady have reunited you, so you know."

A hand touched her shoulder and she turned to see Juana.

"You were mending," Juana spoke, "while the council met. There are those who would stay here and make a home here. It is hidden and the game is plentiful. But the majority wish to know your thoughts. I told them there were people you wished to find."

Alethea nodded. She wished to find many people—Eramaus, Emelye, Darian, Anchises, Boreas, Ada Mos. But those people, she knew, were not the ones Juana had mentioned. It was not time to find her other friends yet. Soon it would be time, but not quite yet.

Juana politely cleared her throat.

Alethea shook away those thoughts and pinned the broach to her breast band close to her heart. "As much as this place feels like home to me," she smiled sadly, one hand on the broach, "we should move as soon as we can. The group of Night and Light living together were north, just on the other side of the ~Pass~. I hope they will be my final clue in how to bring our peoples together so I can lead us out."

ℂℂℂ

It had taken longer to restock supplies than Alethea expected. It was hard to hunt in a drizzle, but at last they were leaving. She was finishing tying up her bedroll when Juana came to her, Maria's father trailing nervously behind her. Maria. A band tightened in Alethea's chest. The girl was not amoung the few children here. Surely she would be safe, even with Lara and Brisa leading.

Juana urged him forward.

"Where is Maria?" Alethea asked, her hand reaching out to touch his shoulder.

"She stayed with Matriarch Amadora. Will you keep her safe Lady?" His eyes glanced up at her.

Alethea shook her head. "I am not The Lady, just Alethea. I am sure Amadora will keep Maria safe." She looked to Juana, who nodded. "But I will pray to The Lady for you."

The man swallowed and nodded. He turned as if to leave, when Juana caught him. "Tell her what you told me."

He turned back, keeping his eyes downcast, speaking haltingly as if unused to being heard. "My brother, he spoke of a place, where men were treated better, and not all women fought."

"Did he say where?" Alethea asked, hope sparking in her

heart.

"Across the Burnt Valley, in the lands of Carlit, tucked into a nook in the northern Dark Barrier."

Alethea glanced to Juana. That matched what she'd seen in her vision.

"We have a few from the Carlit tribe with us," Juana stated. "They may be able to help, but it will depend on how much these people want to be found."

Alethea nodded and glanced to the man again. He worried his hands, and she took them in her own to still them.

"What is your name?"

"Mateo, La, Aletia."

"Mateo," she repeated his name. "Thank you for telling me. You have confirmed a vision I was given. I trust The Lord and The Lady will guide us to them." She smiled as he glanced into her eyes. "May The Lady enlighten you and reunite you with those you love."

He nodded and hurried to shoulder his pack as Alethea shouldered hers. She paused for a moment, looking back at the valley she was certain she was born in. Glancing to her father's resting place, she gave one final silent farewell, before hurrying to catch up to Juana.

They reached the banks of the Pass long before noon as storm clouds began to roll in. They didn't cross it immediately, instead following along it northward, always remaining hidden.

"Never know when the Light might be rumbling through," Coleta whispered jovially.

Alethea nodded. She wanted to see a caravan rumble through. Just seeing the wagon ruts and pony prints in the sand made her miss home. Her heart ached for those she'd come to think of as friends.

"Down!"

The hushed command was passed along and they all

dropped. Silence settled and Alethea swore she heard ponies and the creak of wagons. Unconsciously she began to creep forward, until Coleta's hand caught hers.

"Light will likely kill looking even more like one of us," Juana hissed.

"They don't kill," Salina commented. "Didn't you do a Burnt Valley...." Her voice trailed off at Juana's glare.

"We spar." Colete's light-hearted voice broke the silence. "The Light drop some goods and we retreat. Once they are passed, we pick up what they leave."

"They leave things for you?" Alethea spoke without meaning too. She'd never heard of a payment being given to the Night before.

But before anyone could answer, a rumbling thunder heralded the downpour. Still, they moved forward now, descending into the Pass before the slope became a slippery mess. Alethea paused in the middle. She couldn't see the top of the Pass due to the rain. But northward, down to the side of Theodorio where she grew up, Alethea could see sunlight shining into the jungle beyond the black rocks.

Someday, she thought as she did her best to climb up the other side, The Dark Barrier / Dead Zone would no longer be needed. Someday, there would be no Night or Light, just one people, in a different land.

Chapter 18

❧

It wasn't until they were headed up the pass that Eramaus noticed the two peaks to the south were smoking. He wished Emelye was here. She would have something to say about it. He dropped back to Basil and Giles. They gave him a questioning look and he gestured to the smoking mountains.

"Well, that's new," Giles remarked.

"When the mountains steam, and the springs run dry, you will know that the end of the beginning is nigh," Basil muttered.

Eramaus nodded. His gut twisted inside him as he scanned either side of the pass. There was a six-mile stretch at the top where it would be jungle on the banks to either side of them. It was the place where the Night usually attacked. Eramaus wasn't sure why the road had been banked, as if the Light had wanted to tunnel through the land, instead of going over it. For as long as he could see them Eramaus kept glancing to the smoking mountains. A loud rumble of thunder echoed across the land as rain poured down, limiting all sight.

Boreas rode back to them. "Ya catch tha smoke?"

"Aye," Basil spoke as Giles and Eramaus nodded.

"Got a bad feelin' about it. So we ain't stopping long for lunch. Make sure the goods drop."

Eramaus nodded as Basil responded, "We will."

Swallowing his own bad feeling, Eramaus walked a little faster to check on the goods they would need to heave over. It was secure and wouldn't fall out without help. The whole point of the ruse, he supposed.

As Boreas mentioned, they did not stop long for lunch. Eramaus was trying to help Basil undo the knots when the first arrow hit the canvas.

There was a cry of pain, and Boreas's voice cut in. "MOVE, DOWN, DOWN, DOWN!"

Thwack!

An arrow brushed Eramaus's elbow.

There was another scream.

"They're shooting to kill!" someone shouted as the pace picked up.

"Get this dang thing off!"

Giles was running behind, trying to reach the wagon.

"GET IN AND GET DOWN!" Boreas shouted, he was closer now.

Another arrow pierced the canvas by Basil. The man winced.

"Come on, come on,"

Eramaus looked up when Giles screamed. The man stumbled forward, an arrow in his back.

"I got ye!" Boreas came around with his pony.

"Done!" Basil pronounced, "heave it!"

He and Eramaus heaved the bundle off the wagon as Boreas called strange words into the pouring rain, scooping up the fading Giles.

Eramaus held on tight to the wagon as it picked up speed and watched horrified as an arrow sailed toward the Captain.

"WATCH OUT!"

Boreas's horse jumped the bundle of goods, and Boreas's winced as the arrow hit his side.

"Lord of Light!" the words flung themselves from Eramaus, "Protect them!"

There was an odd drop in the air, making his ears pop. Arrows continued to rain, but they bounced off a barrier. Warriors jumped into the ravine of the pass, running at them. The wagons picked up speed, Boreas on his pony faster still.

"HAIT!"

The woman in the front raised her spear high and hit the ground. Eramaus met the woman's eyes and his blood ran cold. Her staff dropped and a warrior next to her handed her a bow and arrow. She aimed, smiled, and let it loose. Eramaus knew he needed to move, knew it was aimed for his heart. She was Alethea, but not Alethea, and their eyes were locked.

"Eramaus!"

Basil pulled him down, the arrow hitting his shoulder. But he couldn't break the stare. The woman threw back her head and laughed as she shouted to them. He shivered, Basil pulling him further in. *Lord?* Eramaus looked up at the canvas covering. All the arrowheads appeared to point at him. He hugged himself, even as the pain of the arrow fought for his thoughts.

"She, she was," he stumbled with his words later that night as he sat by Basil, while Boreas and Giles were being bandaged properly, "like Alethea, but, but older. Hardened. As if all the goodness had been leached from her and given to Thea. I…"

Basil nudged Eramaus's good shoulder. "It'll be all right."

But it wasn't. They'd lost two of the ponies, and three of the men. The sky poured as if to shed its own tears as they limped into Chuika. Boreas conducted his business as fast as he could. Dusk approached on their second day there and the ponies became restless. They whinnied and kicked their doors. Chickens squawked and the roosters crowed. There was a crash, and a stampede of hogs ran through the streets.

The ground rocked, tossing Eramaus into the side of a building. He winced as his injured shoulder hit it. A red haze lit the sky in the south south-east, followed by a low thunderous growl, though there was not a cloud in the sky. People cried out as the ground rolled under foot like waves on the ocean. Eramaus used the building to balance, turning fearfully to the red haze, wishing he hadn't.

The Holy Land peak spewed black smoke and fire.

ဆာ

The council grumbled about letting a man lead. Coleta, who was also from Carlit, and Alethea walked beside him, stopping with him as they came upon the Dark Barrier for the third time in two days.

"I know they are here." His voice was quiet.

"Aye," Coleta nodded, "I remember stories about them when I was little."

Alethea placed a hand on his shoulder. He was a bit like herself, unsure of being able to lead. "Knowing what I know of both Night and Light, they probably don't want to be found."

"They are watching us," Salina said as she glanced around the trees behind them.

"I agree," Juana stated.

Alethea glanced back at the people they were leading. It was a mix of families, and there was no way she could just bring them back to her home. A home that was no longer hers. She wondered if Eramaus's mother would consent to giving them shelter. Even after four days of rest, everyone was tired. They needed a place to make a home. They should have stayed where Alethea was certain she had been born.

Turning to the trees, Alethea gazed into their boughs. She remembered how the Night had leapt out of them and ran the first day she'd ventured into the Holy Land. Her skin prickled.

"Where do you think they are," she whispered to Salina.

"I have eyes on one, there," Coleta answered, her finger pointing from her side.

Alethea followed it and pin-pointed where it seemed as if someone was watching. There was a shift in the trees, and more became visible. Sensing the women prickling behind her, she motioned for them to relax as she stepped forward, keeping her eyes on the first person spotted. They might actually be male. Male or female, it didn't matter.

Alethea stepped forward again. "~I am Alethea, born of the Night, blessed by the Light. My friends and I seek refuge.~" She spoke in Light then switched back to Night and repeated her words.

"~Prove it~." A male voice from a closer tree spoke in Light.

Alethea turned her attention to that tree. "~And how would you like me to do that? Currently, I have been with the Night, thus I am dressed as the Night. But I grew up among the Light.~"

"And where," a female voice came from the first tree, "did you learn to speak Night?"

"I have listened and learned and was taught by the people you see beside me," she replied.

"Wait, you didn't speak Night before you came to us?" Coleta exclaimed.

"Coleta," Salina hissed, and Alethea was certain she elbowed the woman.

There were two thuds as the man and women hopped down. Alethea stood her ground as they approached. She smiled when she saw that the man carried a staff, while the woman carried a sword. She smiled more realizing that the woman was from the Light and the man from the Night.

"~You are not surprised by us?~" The woman switched to

Light, taking in Alethea and her companions.

Alethea glanced to the sky. "~The Lord and The Lady have called me to unite our peoples. They gave me a vision of a small group where both live in harmony. So I have come to find you and learn what brings you together.~"

The man snorted. "~Then why bring so many with you?~"

Alethea looked back at the others. Their faces were curious, the man who had been leading them was hopeful. Juana's brows were furrowed, and Alethea remembered the girl had been learning Light. Her eye's caught Alethea's and she nodded. Alethea turned back to the man and woman.

"~You may not have seen the mountains smoke, or felt the earth quake, but there is change coming to this land, for the leaders of both the Night and the Light are not making the right choices. These people are fleeing because they would be persecuted by the new leaders of the Night.~"

"We have seen Palos on fire, but the earth has not—"

The ground heaved beneath them. Alethea's arms flailed out as she heard the man and woman panicking. They tried to run. But the shifting earth tripped them.

And then the ground dropped.

People screamed.

"LORD AND LADY PROTECT US!" Alethea grabbed hold of the two strangers, shouting, "Illumine and Enlighten-us!"

And the ground stilled.

Alethea kept hold of the strangers' shoulders. They tottered next to a rift, the smell of rotten eggs seeping from it. Other hands came and helped, moving them away from the ledge. The man and woman looked to each other.

"Both Gods are mad," Alethea said in Night so her group could understand. "What our peoples have done to make them madder than when the Light tried to kill me in the Lady's Tower, I do not know. But your family, your friends," she addressed the two strangers, "may be hurt. I was training to be The Lady of Light. Toli," she gestured to the boy who was already tending to an elder, "is a poporo in training. We will do our part to work and live with you."

"For how long?" the woman asked.

"I do not know," Alethea admitted. "There is much I still have to learn before the path I must lead others on becomes clear."

"I am Urvasi," the woman stated as her companion began to lead them. "And he is Pulido. Welcome to the Zagamilos tribe."

⋐⋑⋐⋑

When Captain Boreas and his crew arrived in Paramythia, the city was in total disarray. Guards made them set up camp outside of town as there was no room in the inns and taverns. Glancing to the skyline of the city that evening, Eramaus noted one of the palace towers had been knocked down. Swiveling, he focused on Archtheos, noting that the Basilica spire was also gone. He smirked. Served them right.

What was not right, he realized the next day, were the common folks cleaning up rubble from the broken homes of counts and dukes. Boreas sent his men out to help with clean up. Eramaus stuck with Giles and Basil. Between their injuries from the Pass, the three of them managed to muster the strength and ability of two men.

They stumbled back to their camp that night, bone weary. Giles and Basil turned in quickly, but Eramaus wandered to the edge of camp, restless. Two familiar voices by one of the wagons piqued his interest.

"I don't like what's going on," Knight Anchises said.

"Aye, it rubs me bones tha wrong way," Captain Boreas agreed.

"The Lady Daphne is doing what she can, but the new

Empress has her claws in our new Emperor so subtly I doubt he even knows she's pulling the strings. Only two of the force sent into the Holy Land came back, and they only lived long enough to tell us that all the Night were dead."

"All the Night?" Eramaus stepped around the corner, his heart beating fast.

The two turned to him. Boreas furrowed his brows and opened his mouth, but Anchises held up his hand.

"Our Lady wasn't among them. Darian was able to glean that much."

Eramaus relaxed slightly. And then asked, "Do you think the Night know?"

"Eramaus, ye need to get rest," Boreas chided him.

"But—"

"What's your concern, lad?" Anchises interrupted.

"They attacked us in the pass, shot to kill," he gestured to his shoulder and then to the bandage around Boreas's waist. "They've only ever attacked with staves, never with bows and spears. I mean, the two times I—"

"Tha lad's right," Boreas interrupted. "But they attacked what," the Captain counted on his fingers, "two, no, three days before the earth quaked. Which I presume marked tha attack on tha Holy Land."

Anchises nodded consent.

"So, they didn't know." Not that it made Eramaus feel better. "But the twin peaks are also smoking, or were when we went through the Pass. Do you think The Lady of Night is not happy as well?"

Both of them studied him and once more the prophecy came to mind. "Take heart those who do not doubt, for one will be chosen to lead you out." His brows furrowed and he looked down. "Heed the child of the Night, blessed by the Light," he strained his memory, "for she will guide you as our Gods reunite." Triumphant, he raised his head, glancing at the men. "Thea Lady must be the chosen one. She will lead us out. And I don't think it will just be us, not if the Gods reunite. It must be Light *and* Night. That's why—"

"Well, no one be leadin' no one right now," Boreas interrupted. "Not in this mess," he sighed.

Anchises was silent for a long moment, studying Eramaus. "Listen," he turned back to the Captain, "as I said, the new Empress is manipulating things to her liking. She's married off the old Empress to her own father. And after that eruption, he's in a hurry to send Princess Eris to Valaora over the Pass. And as the Knight assigned to his princedom, I've been assigned to escort her and Prince Lyrcus—"

"I have to go," Eramaus interjected. "I promised Thea Lady, I'd protect Lyrcus. I've been horrible at it. I *have* to do this."

This time, both Anchises and Boreas studied him. Eramaus met their gazes in equal turns. Finally, he could do what he was supposed to be doing.

At last, Anchises nodded. "If you can spare him," Anchises turned to Boreas, "I would feel better having another I trust with us. The insistence we go over the Pass, combined with the mercenaries that have been hired, do not make me feel at ease. I do not understand why they are not sent to Mina to travel back with the Prince on his boat."

"Aye, I'll spare Eramaus." The Captain smiled sadly. "Don't want to, but I can see his mind is set, like it was the day Alethea took to the sea to become a mediki."

A wry grin crossed Anchises's face as he nodded. "Fair." He turned to Eramaus. "I'll ensure you get gear and set Cyrus and Orion to rear guard. Slip in with them as we pass and remain unseen as much as possible from the rest. Change your look if you can."

§ÐCß

Upon arrival in Zagamilos, Alethea's group were given two huts, where occupants had died from a sickness long ago. Toli was asked to cleanse it, and Alethea helped as best she could. Juana stood outside for a long time, even after the others had gone in. Salina tried to coax her in, while Coleta dared her to enter. It wasn't until Alethea placed a hand on Juana's arm that the young woman's stare broke.

Juana smiled sadly, whispering, "I lost my family in the same sickness." Alethea squeezed her arm, and Jauna's smile grazed her as she turned to the others. "Can a woman not get lost in thought, or do we only let men do that?"

Being given an 'unclean' hut should have been Alethea's first clue that they weren't welcome. It wouldn't be the last one either. Everyone in their group who could, took on a role to help the village. Juana, Salina and two others joined the hunting parties. They brought in some of the best kills, yet took home the worst of the meat. Four of their men joined in to help with the gardens. Their patches thrived, yet they brought back the least of the harvest. Even in the healing hut, where Alethea and Toli spent their time, little was given to them in return for their service. It was made worse when they forbade Alethea from calling upon either God to save a hunter from dying.

Given the last few months, feeling like and being treated like a threatening stranger had become a facet of her life. But for the Night she had led there, the lack of respect and welcoming irked them. It was a constant morning complaint made before they went to their respective tasks.

"Welcome to my life," Alethea muttered, perhaps a little too loud, as she passed by a small knot of women.

"Welcome? To your life?" one of the women disbelievingly repeated. "And why haven't you done anything about it? You are *the chosen*, are you not?"

Alethea stopped. "So I am led to believe." She turned to the small group. "Though being chosen, seems to also make me the outcast, the one looked down upon. And it feels as though you all," she gestured broadly to all of them, "have been brought into it by being here with me. That was not my intent."

"And your intent was?"

"To see how people of the Night and Light could live together."

"And how's that gone?"

"It's given me a headache trying to figure it out," she sighed. "Now, I must go to the healing homes and, as always, do my best to fit in where I am not wanted." Alethea plastered a smile on her face, nodded, and left.

It was a bit rankling to only be allowed to mix healing concoctions as directed by others, when she could call upon The Lord and The Lady to heal people fully. They disliked her calling upon one of the Gods, let alone both of them. People were expected to suffer their injuries and mend as the natural course of things. It felt very much like a Night perspective.

But, Alethea had not tended the injured in Archtheos. Perhaps the Light felt the same, and it was only her friends who found her healing to their liking. Alethea paused in her preparations of a herbal concoction to look toward the willow tree. *Why* am *I here*, she thought, *if not to learn how Night and Light can live together?*

Not how, the wind whispered in two giggling harmonious voices.

Then what?

To learn, began the deeper voice.

That your task, the higher voice continued.

Is not impossible, they finished together as the wind ruffled her hair.

Right, Alethea turned back to her task. *As not impossible as it will be to find ships to sail us all over the seas. Whoever all of us ends up being.*

Chapter 19

༒

The next day, Eramaus transformed at the hands of Basil and Giles. It was oddly heartbreaking to see all of his deep purple hair on the ground after they nearly shaved his head. Eramaus hadn't been at all sure about having his eyebrows reshaped, but Giles insisted it was quite effective. Lastly, the mercenary kolobus and leather armor he'd gotten from Boreas was changed to something from another company. It barely fit, showing off his outer thigh.

Struggling to pull it closed, he missed Anchises's passage. But it was hard to miss the opulent carriage. He blinked at it. How was he supposed to hide in a wagon train that only had two wagons and a carriage? A ten-wagon caravan like Count Manella's was much easier to hide in.

Sighing, he watched the lavish carriage roll by, its tiny wheels bouncing on the hard dirt road. How it would fare on the rougher road of the Pass, he didn't know. Three squires, along with five mercenaries, marched behind it. He recognized squire Hector, who didn't even glance his way, but none of the others. The second wagon was followed by more mercenaries, and Eramaus quickly glanced at anything but them. One of them was the man who had pushed him and Emelye off the road. No wonder Anchises was worried. Finally the last wagon rolled by, pulled four straining ponies. Cyrus and Orion marched behind it.

With one last effort to close his kolobus, Eramaus marched just faster than the caravan, before falling into step between Cyrus and Orion.

"Nice thighs," Cyrus winked at him.

"Not my fault they didn't give me gear that fits," Eramaus muttered.

Cyrus grinned. "Great to have your grumpiness with us, Mause."

Eramaus furrowed his brows with a glance at the man.

"Aye, Mause," Orion echoed. "Good to know we've got another on our side."

Eramaus nodded, letting it sink in that he was going to be called Mause.

They stayed at the Duke's houses in Forma and Chuika before setting up a fancy camp at the bottom of the Pass. Anchises directed the loads of the carts and wagon to be distributed differently, as well as insisting the carriage wheels were strengthened, despite the former Empress's protests about how ugly they looked.

"With all due respect, Your Highness, the Pass is danger-ous. It is not unknown for the people of Night to attack."

"Attack!" the former empress exclaimed. "But we have a treaty!"

"A treaty that was broken when the emperor attacked the Holy Land, Your Highness. Maybe they do not know of that yet, but it is best we are prepared for the worst."

She continued to gripe, but movement out of the corner of Eramaus's eye caught his attention. Prince Lyrcus was not good at leaving stealthily. Or maybe it was just Eramaus's practice at sneaking away from his brothers that made the boy easy to spot. Still, Eramaus hadn't been able to approach the prince yet, and he needed Prince Lyrcus to know he was there. That he hadn't forgotten what Thea had told him to do.

Stopping just beyond the edge of camp, Prince Lyrcus gazed up into the Dead Zone. Eramaus made some noise so as not to startle the young prince as he walked up, stopping next to him.

"Are you going to insist I go back?" he asked in annoyance. "I am perfectly safe here. No Night would attack here, would they?"

"No, they would not," Eramaus assured him. "Your Highness."

The boy sighed. "Do you think we'll see the Night up there?"

"I hope we don't."

"But it's their lands."

"Yes, it is, your Highness. We are trespassers on it, and I don't think they are happy with how that's been going."

The prince finally turned to him. The boy's brows furrowed, and his eyes narrowed. Eramaus briefly met his gaze before turning back to gaze at the Dead Zone and the road that went up it.

"I feel like I've met you before. What's your name?"

"Mause, your Highness," Eramaus replied.

"No, I'm certain that's not it. It's more than," his words were cut by his sharp intake of breath. His hand went to Eramaus's arm. "You're Squire Eramaus!"

"I am not a squire any longer, Prince Lyrcus." He turned to face the boy. "But I am here to protect you as I was told I should. I am sorry I ran the day the Tower fell."

"Well, that is all right, they would have hauled you off anyway. But, but I thought my brother was going to have you killed. I told him he really shouldn't. And then he started asking why *I* was—"

Eramaus put a finger to the boy's lips. "We should not talk of such things. I just wanted you to know the Pass is dangerous, and I will protect you as long as I am able."

The boy's brows furrowed again, and he touched the bandage on Eramaus's left shoulder.

Eramaus glanced at it. "A wound from the last time I went through the Pass. The Night are restless, and I hope we see none."

Prince Lyrcus turned back to the Pass. "I just, they say," his voice went quiet and Eramaus stepped closer to hear him, "that the, The Lady Alethea is dead. Do you, do you believe that?"

"I did," Eramaus confirmed. He studied where the green of the rainforest above the black rock was slowly turning into a dark outline against the evening sky, and felt the prince's eyes on him.

"But now you do not?"

"I," Eramaus stopped, "I think my cousin Emelye put it best." A smile flitted across his face. "Why would The Lord of Light ensure she lived through multiple assassination attempts to have her die now?" He brought his focus back to the prince. "I think she is with the Night, trying to find allies, as she did among us. After all, we must heed the child of the Night, blessed by the Light, for she will guide us as *our* Gods reunite."

℠⛎ℝ

Juana intercepted Alethea on her way back from the healing home. The council had met without her, again. However, Juana told Alethea, they wanted to return to the place they had found Alethea's father. There was shelter, which could be expanded. It was off the paths and hidden. Not to mention, there was plenty to hunt and gather. And the group had leaders, hunters, cooks, and even healers. They saw no reason not to make it their home as these people had made Zagamilos theirs. Alethea agreed.

She'd gained no insight in Zagamilos. And though she ached for the sea, knew she needed to lead them to the sea, she had no idea how to convince them to go. Let alone how to bring so many Night through the land of the Light to get to there.

Gathering what little resources they'd been given, they left the next morning, reaching the Pass just before nightfall. Half of them wanted to cross, but Alethea and Juana agreed with the council—it would be better to stay in the trees. There were too many signs of the place being occupied recently. Settling into her hammock high in a tree, Alethea gazed north down the Pass. It was strewn with black rocks. Some she could pinpoint where they had been pried from the Dark Barrier.

Alethea held onto her branch and leaned over her hammock's edge to where Juana, Coleta, and Salina were. "Is it me," she whispered, "or are they starting to barricade off the ~Pass~, Burnt Valley?"

"You are worried?" Juana asked quietly as Salina began to ascend the tree.

Alethea nodded. "We have to get down there eventually. Sooner, rather than later."

It wasn't long before Salina came back, face grim. "It's not totally blocked, but it's definitely not big enough for those beasts and things the Light use to cross."

"~Wagons~," Alethea supplied the word even as she sighed. "I don't like this." She locked eyes with Juana. "We need to go below the Dark Barrier before the way is impassable or we cannot go into the sun."

Juana nodded. "I'll let the council know so they can start stewing over it now." She swung off, over to another tree.

"How do you expect us to travel through the land of the

Light?" Salina asked as she returned to her hammock. "If they had issues with you, won't it be worse for us?"

"I know." Alethea sighed. "I'm not sure yet, but there are places with few people, and the Night are used to traveling on smaller paths than the Light." She smiled slightly. "I think it would be easier than getting the Light through the Land of the Night. Your ~roads~ are barely a person wide."

Salina chuckled as she ensconced herself in her hammock.

Alethea continued watching the way Juana went until she got back.

"It's going to take them a while to get used to the idea," Juana stated.

"I know." Alethea's gaze found the smoking twin peaks outlined in black against the setting sun. "But I don't think the Gods are giving us much of a choice."

Waking to storm clouds dimming the light of dawn, a sense of foreboding filled her. She felt as though she was moving through a thick soup. She wasn't the only one to be slow. A heavy silence pervaded the group. They crept cautiously toward the edge of the Pass. For all she tried, Alethea could not call it the Burnt Valley as the Night did, though she preferred Dark Barrier to Dead Zone.

Juana sent Salina ahead to scout and they all waited, listening to the drums.

"They are watching a group of Light," Coleta muttered.

Juana sighed. "Toli, what time of day is it?"

"Near halfway through," Toli responded.

"Come on, Salina," Juana hissed. "If we don't move soon, we'll need to,"

Lightning lit the sky, echoing thunder drowning out Juana's words and anxiety stirred in Alethea's gut.

"There she is," Juana let out a breath. "Let's go, everyone cross."

Staring up the Pass as Juana ushered people over, Alethea

remained where she was until all had crossed but her and Juana.

"Come on, we need to cross." Juana urged her down the bank.

They were almost across when a crack echoed against the banks.

"Come on," Juana urged her.

But Alethea was frozen, staring at the opulent carriage listing to one side. Drums beat, and a single word broke the silence.

"MARK!"

"No!" Alethea gasped as the sound of fighting began. "No, no, no."

She ran toward the carriage before anyone could stop her.

⚜

Storm clouds ran to meet them as they trudged up the slope of the Pass. The moment he saw the trees, Eramaus focused on them, trying to see the Night hiding in them. As they neared the top, a drum echoed beside them. It beat a measure, then stopped. Further down the Pass, another drum repeated that measure. Anchises only stopped at the top long enough to distribute food, and they continued on, eating as they went. Eramaus could hear the former empress complaining about it.

He strained his eyes as another drum beat out a measure. It came from the other side of the Pass, and a little behind them. Once more, the drums ahead of them repeated its measure.

Eramaus gripped the hilt of his sword. "It started with arrows," He said softly to Cyrus and Orion as they began the descent down the other side.

The wind picked up as the sky darkened. Every muscle

in Eramaus's body tensed, like a rabbit ready to move at any sight of danger. His hand itched to draw his sword to be ready. But what did a sword do against arrows? His eyes constantly scanned the trees, the banks, waiting, listening.

Lightning lit the sky as the thunder made all of them jump. The following silence was deafening, until a crack and high-pitched squeal broke it.

Everyone rushed forward to where the opulent carriage listed heavily to one side, its right front wheel broken.

"Get them out, get that wheel fixed," Knight Anchises ordered.

Eramaus helped Lyrcus, but as a mercenary, he was ordered to the wheel. Even as he helped, he tried to keep an eye on the prince. Hector, Cyrus and Orion stood by the boy and his mother. The Knight sat on his pony, making a slow circle to watch the banks and trees.

A drum began to beat.

"MARK!"

That one word, spoken by an unknown squire, unleashed confusion.

Anchises was thrown from his screaming pony. Mercenaries attacked Hector, Orion, and Cyrus. The carriage dropped its full weight on Eramaus. Thunder rumbled in the sky.

Eramaus roared, pushing his way out from under the carriage. He ignored the pain in his shoulder as he drew his sword. His first slash ripped into the side of a mercenary. The man turned and Eramaus slit his throat. Bile burned his mouth, but he'd broken their wall.

"Out!" Anchises cried above the steel and thunder.

THWACK! Thunk, th-thunk thunk.

Arrows echoed on the wood. Ponies screamed and wagons jolted.

"SET."

It was the same voice that started the chaos, and Eramaus

swung as the man passed him by.

Another volley of arrows rained down as the former empress screamed.

Eramaus ducked under the shields his fellow squires held over Prince Lyrcus and his mother. The carriage behind them jolted forward, digging deeper into the ground.

"We need to fight them!" Prince Lyrcus demanded.

"Too many," Cyrus spoke, as Eramaus restrained the boy.

"We're going to die," Empress Eris whimpered.

Another volley of arrows thudded against the shields.

Orion dashed to Anchises as the man yelped.

"Lord of Light, set protection around us!"

Eramaus lifted his glowing sword, pointing it skyward, drawing a large circle encompassing them all. Bright fire flared up, leaving a glowing line around them. Arrows rained down, burning into ash before they reached them.

"Holy fire?" Cyrus breathed, easing up on the crouching.

"How long will it last?" Orion limped over with Anchises.

"Till attacks wear it down." Anchises leaned heavily on Orion. They all watched Night descending from the Pass walls, Not-Thea in the lead. "Know how strong your spell is?"

Eramaus shook his head. "I dispelled it last time."

Lightning lit the sky again, as thunder shook the ground. The Night paused, Not-Thea urging them on. They balked as another bolt struck a tree, splitting it in two. Still, Not-Thea moved forward, her eyes burning with hatred.

Chapter 20

Alethea saw the ring of protection go up. "Eramaus." His name passed as a whispered prayer. She watched arrows rain upon it, disintegrating into ash at its touch. Night began to pour from the banks of the Pass. They carried spears, yelled to kill. There were not enough Light to provide a defense.

"Aletia!" Juana tried to grab her. "We can't fight them. There are too many!"

The air crackled and tingled, filling Alethea with power. Too many, not enough, one sided, always running. It was unfair! She reached out, the lightning begging her to use it.

"Strike by them, Lord / Lady," she hissed. "Make *them* run!"

Lightning struck near the Night, but their leader urged them forward.

"Lord / Lady!" She would make it to the caravan. "Make them fear as *I* have feared!"

Once more, the sky unleashed its fury, taking a tree with it. The Night balked. The smallest of them glanced to Alethea before urging their companions to back away, leaving their leader alone.

"Brisa," Coleta snarled from beside Alethea.

Brisa was the woman who'd killed the Gran Mamara. Brisa was the one that killed the Empress sixteen years ago. But it was the look on the woman's face that dredged up memories. Memories that had been buried deep, until she'd found her parents' cave.

"BRISA!" Jauna's voice carried across the pass.

Alethea barely noticed Salina join Coleta and Juana at her side as Brisa turned her hatred on them.

"BRISA," Juana continued, "you *will* let those Light go!"

"I will let no Burnt Demons go!" Brisa screamed back to them. "I will kill you and them, as soon as I kill that burnt spawn of a demon, like I killed her mother!"

❧❧

The moment Not-Thea's focus shifted, Anchises commanded them to climb through the broken caravan.

"We'll die getting through the barrier," Hector stated.

"You said you can dispel it?" Anchises addressed Eramaus as they followed the weeping former empress.

"Did before."

They stopped. Lyrcus was trying to urge his mother to continue, but she remained frozen. Orion's hands were on the reins.

"There's another group of Night," Lyrcus said, as Cyrus hefted the Empress onto a pony.

"Then we will gallop through them," Anchises growled. "But we need to get *off* their Land."

"But the, the, false Lady," Eris whimpered.

"Thea?" Eramaus leapt down, eyes finding the other group that Not-Thea now faced.

Alethea stood, barely covered in the clothing of the Night, facing Not-Thea. A short version of the Night's long staff held across her body, the ferocity of her face chilling him. Light flickered from Thea's fingertips as a bolt of lightning toppled a tree. Three Night stood by her. One he recognized as the girl who had thanked him, what felt like a lifetime ago. The second was slender, a bow in her hands. The third was the biggest woman Eramaus had ever seen.

"Eramaus!" Anchises's voice brought him back to his group. "Mount and drop that barrier!"

Eramaus mounted the remaining pony, his eyes flicking again to Thea. Not-Thea had locked eyes on her, the three Night making a semi-circle of protection around her. The ponies pawed the ground as Anchises muttered soft incantations of protection.

~HAIT~" someone called from the trees.

Not-Thea whipped around, shouting to the other Night. The group around Thea broke into a run northwards as Eramaus's pony reared.

"Eramaus," Cyrus shouted, "release your protection. NOW."

"Lord of Light," Eramaus spoke loudly, "release the barrier!"

His ears popped as they spurred their ponies to a run. Glancing to Thea, he saw her stumble and watched as the big woman scooped her up before Eramaus could make it there.

℘)ℭ

Alethea felt Brisa's hatred. It radiated like a funeral pyre, burning hotter and hotter as the woman stormed closer.

"Let it go," Alethea commanded.

"He stole her from me," Brisa spat out with each step. "He destroyed our plans. And I will destroy—"

"HAIT!" A voice that sounded like Tara's called from the trees.

The Night on the banks, trying to avoid the falling trees, ran.

"I DID NOT CALL OUT A RETREAT!" Brisa spun back to face the trees.

"Run. Now!" Juana hissed.

They complied, but a voice pulled Alethea's attention to the Light. Eramaus? Where'd his hair go? She stumbled, and as Coleta scooped her up, Alethea recognized Anchises and the others on ponies.

"Follow them!" She pointed as they all raced down the hill.

"~Help them!~" She heard Eramaus call out.

"Trust—" Alethea began, her words turning into a scream as pain shot through her.

"THEA!" Eramaus's voice tore at her heart.

She fought for consciousness, aware of Coleta transferring her to Eramaus's pony.

"I'll get Toli," Coleta hollered as she veered from them.

Their ride flashed in and out of darkness. Alethea was aware of Juana leaping on behind Eramaus, trying to give directions. Anchises, unwavering in getting them off the Night's lands. The rocks she'd seen strewn in the Pass loomed tall. Then it was the trees that loomed, and black rocks. They stopped, and she let the darkness take her.

Chapter 21

Eramaus held tight to Alethea, barely aware of Juana behind him, her voice forceful as she tried to shout directions. Anchises either didn't hear her or ignored her. Either way, Eramaus's pony didn't want to do anything except follow the others as they plunged around the black rocks strewn across the Pass.

Down they went, at full gallop, till Anchises veered them into the rainforest. They crashed through the brush, weaving past trees, till Anchises called out to halt. The Dead Zone rose steeply beside them, water running down its face into a small stream.

"Off the beasts and let them go," Anchises commanded.

Cyrus took Alethea gently from Eramaus. Juana was already on the ground, approaching Anchises, the slender Night woman bristling beside her. Cyrus laid Alethea on her side, a spear sticking out just below her ribs.

Eramaus knelt beside her. "Thea." He took her hand is his own, but she didn't respond. "Thea, you can't die. You're not supposed to die."

Hector knelt on Thea's other side. "That's not good."

"We should take it out," Cyrus stated, kneeling as well.

"We should wait." Anchises came back to them, Juana by his side. "Orion and the other Night one is fetching…" he looked to Juana.

"Toli. He is ~poporo~," she stated in Light as if that should explain everything.

"Toli," Eramaus spoke the name without meaning to. He wasn't supposed to tell anyone about that day when he met the Night in the Holy Land. *Forgive me Thea, they need to know,* he thought. "He's like, a mediki, I think. He helped Thea Lady when she was stabbed, in the Holy Land."

He felt Anchises's gaze. He'd told the Knight Thea had healed herself. Eramaus swallowed.

"We need," Juana continued in her broken Light, "take out spear. Might have…." her face screwed up for a moment, "bad on it."

They all tore strips from their kolobus, handing them to Eramaus. Cyrus held Thea's body steady as Hector straddled her, hands on the spear shaft next to her skin.

"One," he counted.

Eramaus squeezed Thea's hand as thunder rumbled over the treetops.

"Two."

Rain began to drip through the leaves as Eramaus readied to apply the first bandage.

"Three!"

Hector yanked the spear out.

Lightning ripped through the trees as Thea screamed into the thunder.

CRACK! Thunk. A tree fell near them as Eramaus applied pressure on the wound.

Lord, don't let her die, please, Eramaus begged, noting the black blood on the spearhead, and Juana's deep frown. *Please, I will do anything to have her live.*

Anything? the wind whispered about him, almost feminine in its tone.

Anything! he cried back, switching one bandage for another as squires fought the wind to get a tarp over them.

Call upon us both. Promise us that she will be your Lady, mother to all, wife of none, till at last from the Godly fire your journey has begun.

How was he to know when that journey would begin, how was he to—

"She's not breathing." Hector tried to roll her to her back, the thunder fading into the distance.

Call on us and Promise! the wind called, two voices in one.

"I can't feel or hear a heartbeat."

The rain stopped, as Juana yelled something in Night, turning to the sound of a galloping horse.

Promise. The wind whipped about Eramaus.

"I promise!" he cried out, "JUST HEAL HER."

He shot his arms into the air, hoping to gather light as Thea always did. "Heal her." He brought his hand down, tipping it, but no light poured from it.

CALL BOTH OF US, the wind roared in his ears.

"Lord of Light and Lady of Night," Eramaus threw his hand up again, "heal her and she will remain Thea Lady for as long as you like." Light flowed into his hand. "Illumine-her!"

"Enlighten-her," Toli prayed, settling on his knees across from Eramaus

Silver and gold light poured from them both onto Alethea. She convulsed, her body jerking as she shifted onto her back and gasped for breath. Tears ran down Eramaus's face as he slumped back. Toli fell over, caught by Juana. And then, Thea's eyes blinked open, catching his.

~Eramaus?~ Her soft voice seemed to be in his mind, her lips barely moving.

"I'm here, Thea," he whispered, once more taking her hand in his own. ~I'm here,~ he thought, as his own eyes closed with hers and darkness enveloped them.

Lament Verse 3

Alethea

I've found friends among the Night,
their hearts are true and their spirits bright.
Though not all the Night do wish me well,
to some I am a spawn of hell.
And now I see from both sides,
In any heart hate can reside.
Reunited with my love at last,
I know I can move us from this past.

Eramaus

Taught from birth to hate the Night,
I always thought that might was right.
But in my love, both sides reside,
Night and Light in compromise.
Though others may be fraught with greed,
To be with my love is all I need.
But war has come, and all must fight,
or from this isle we must take flight.

May
The Lord of Light Illumine-You
and
The Lady of Night Enlighten-You

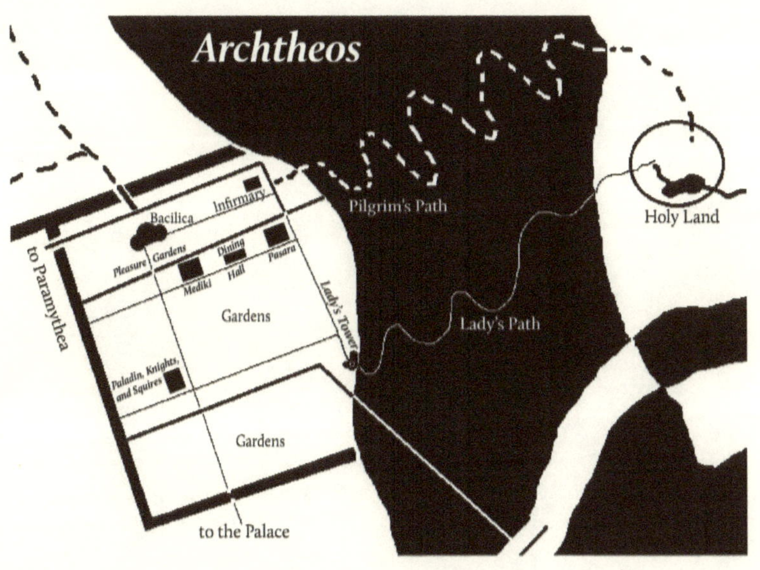

Archtheos
Pilgrim's Path
Holy Land
Infirmary
Bacilica
Pleasure Gardens
Mediki
Dining Hall
Pasara
to Paramythea
Gardens
Lady's Tower
Lady's Path
Paladin, Knights, and Squires
Gardens
to the Palace

Acknowledgments

To my coworker, Dana, who loved my books so much she had be a Beta Reader for this book so she could get her fix sooner. She's proved her worth by promptly catching a plot hole when I rearranged the ending.

To Chaos Publications and TheChelle who runs it, thank you for letting me go my own way before veering back to you after Corrugated Sky fell apart. I'm glad to officially be part of The Chaos.

To Write Club and The Old Bay Scribes, together we weathered the November 2023 debacle. Thanks to all your support, this novel is now launching two months ahead of my original schedule schedule.

To the creator of Sprinto, the sprint bot on Discord, all of my novels have been written with your bot's help. From ten minute sprints to power-half-hours, it's always helped keep me focus.

To my family, you are amazing and awesome and I could not ask for a better husband or children. Not only do you give me space to write, you actively support my writing.

About the Author

Peace Forgotten is Cathryn's third novel, which will be followed by one more to wrap up the series.

When she's not writing and publishing her stories, Cathryn manages the quality aspects of a clinical laboratory by day and her husband, two children, and pets by night. Over the course of the years she's used her free time to learn to ride a motorcycle, earn her black belt in karate with her eldest child, and travel the world with her family. Along with these epic endeavors, she experiments with yarn, fabric, and, of course, words.

The Verses of Alethea's Lament:

by Cathryn Leigh

Published

Verse 1: Love Lost

Verse 2: Hope Extinguished

Verse 3: Peace Forgotten

Work In Process

Verse 4: Faith Transformed

www.ingramcontent.com/pod-product-compliance
Lightning Source LLC
Chambersburg PA
CBHW032220190726
48289CB00007BA/2313